# What Peace Means to Us

by

Izaak David Diggs

Released 12 May 2020 (LED)

Library of Congress
ISBN 978-1-7345428-1-3
Registration: TXu002182049

Cover design by Candy Jones
Story prompts for "Rage Room" and "Today's Lesson" also courtesy of Candy Jones

Yes, the lack of page numbers was intentional

what peace means to us what peace means to us what peace means to us what peace means to us what peace means to us what peace means to us what peace means to us what peace means to us

what peace means to us **The Seldom Dogs** to us what peace means to us what peace means to us what peace means to us what peace means to us what peace means to us what peace peace means to us what peace means to us what peace means to us  what peace means to us

# Rage Room to us what peace means to us what peace means to us what peace means to us what peace means to us what peace means to us what peace means to us what peace means to us what peace means to us what peace means to us what peace means to us what peace means to us what peace means to us what peace means to us what peace means to us what peace means to what peace means to us what peace means to us what peace means to us what peace means to us what peace means to us

what peace means to us **Today's Lesson** us what peace means to us what peace means to us what peace means to us what peace means to us what peace means to us what peace means to us what peace means to us what peace means to us what peace means to us what peace means to us what peace means to us what peace means to us what peace means to us what peace means to us what peace means to us what peace means

to us what peace means to us what peace means to **Golden Bullet** means to us what peace means to us what peace means to us what peace means to us what peace means to us what peace means to what peace means to us what peace means to us what peace means to us what peace means to us

us what **Death Becomes Dewy Green** peace means to us what peace means to us what peace means to us what peace means to us what peace means to us what peace means to us what peace means to us what peace means to us what peace

# The Seldom Dogs

# 1

Last night I dreamt that my son was waving. There he was, standing on his own in short grass between two buildings. Was he waving at me? Was he smiling? No--my son was in trouble. I knew what was coming and tried to warn him but was unable to. There I was, standing helpless from a distance I could normally cross in a second--*I can't see this, I can't.*
The dream ended abruptly; I had failed him again.

*You need to talk about it*, that's the thing I hear the most. Talk--picking words from the chaos in my head and making sentences--
I have no idea where to start.
Someone suggested *free association*; just picking the first thing that pops in my head and seeing where it leads.
The first thing that comes to mind are the calendars:
The school emailed one every month to remind us parents about holidays and special events. This month's has a picture of a couple of kids playing catch, not that kids ever seem to play catch anymore. My son wrote "FTP" in the box for today's date; I keep looking at those three letters in his bad handwriting and think about those dreams where he waves that stiff armed wave.

The expression on his face is the worst part, like he has discovered something nasty under a rock, something coiled up and ready to hurt him.

Thinking about my son reminds me of when I was a kid and all the pointless shit they made us do. When I was in school they made us read all these old stories.
There was one about this company that gave guided tours of the past--a really long ago, the time of the dinosaurs.
The big rule was "Don't step off the path; if you step off the path bad shit will happen."
Someone steps off the path and crushes a butterfly. They return to the present and everything is fucked up because of that stupid dead butterfly. That story meant nothing to me as a kid. It was just something they made us read that bored the shit out of us.
Today I would give anything to feel that sort of boredom.
Today, I know what it's like to crush a butterfly.

The day I put the playing catch calendar on the fridge was good: My boy called me 'Dad' for the first time.
I played it cool but inside I nearly lost my shit.
A week after I put that calendar up my son was waving with a look on his face no parent ever wants to see.
Maybe I should have let him live with his grandmother.
He'd been okay, living with assholes but okay--
Instead I insisted that he come live with me--*insisted*.
There is no one I can blame for this but myself.

I was a little older than my son when I went to live with Grandma. No one explained to me what was going on; I thought I was being punished. My dad had already left at that point and my mother was in no condition to look after me. She had whomever she was fucking that week drop me at the bus station:

One suitcase. One backpack. A lot of questions that wouldn't be answered for a long time. I went to live with Grandma and all her rules and chores.

Grandma who would knock on the door if you slept past seven.

Grandma who always found work for you to do.

At the time I hated that shit and had no idea why she was so strict.

At the time I didn't understand that she was just trying to keep me from becoming a fuck up like my parents.

At first I thought that the beginning of this story was when my son came to live with me. Maybe the real beginning is when my Grandma died: It was only when my grandmother died that I could become the person I am.

I took the playing catch calendar off the fridge and went to throw it away.

Pulling it off I froze; it would have been like throwing away part of my son.

I just paced the kitchen with that paper in my hand: Trash? Fridge? Trash?

In the end I put it back on the fridge and stared at the three letters my boy had written.

This must be what it feels like to have a broken heart.

No, this must be what it feels like to have a shattered heart.

I was temping in an office when I made the decision to be a Dad. When I got the text from Noah's mother two details stand out:
A radio playing "Baker Street" by Gerry Rafferty.
A loud woman in the next cubicle talking about back to school shopping.
She was complaining to a co-worker about how much shit costs. In the middle of her bitching about the price of jeans my phone beeped. As I grabbed my mobile Baker Street went into the cheesy sax solo. The caller ID told me it was Cheyenne. Had I missed some child support payments? That was usually the only reason she contacted me so I knew the drill:
Wages garnished, my boss knowing what a fuck up I really am.
I should have known there is no getting off that easy.
My ex had joined some end of the world nuts out in Idaho. Noah didn't like it out there and had been acting up and causing problems. Asking what he had done just pissed his mom off; I could feel the heat coming through my phone--
Bringing up shit from ten years ago, how all this is my fault. Why couldn't she just answer the fucking question?
*Why did you put your dick in that bag of crazy?*
My grandmother's voice, not that she would have used those words.
"If you don't want him, he's going to stay with his Grandma."

Gail: Not just a nut but a Jesus nut. Cheyenne is smarter than me, knows I'd hate Noah living with that crazy hag. I told my ex to put him on a bus. *Insisted.*
Even gave her my debit card info, something I would normally never would trust her with. The conversation ended and the weight of the situation settled on me.
What the hell I had done? I sat in that cubicle clenching my phone, meaningless hard plastic that, with a turn, meant everything.
In a week my son would be coming to live with me.
That was the most scared I've ever felt…
No, there was one other time but this was a close second. Despite my fear there was the understanding that I had to get my shit together to do the right thing; I had to be strong and sane for him just like Grandma was for me. Could I be her equal? Could I stop being a selfish asshole and put my son first?
The doubt I felt made it hard to be optimistic.

My son coming to live with me opened the door to a bunch of shit I don't like to think about. Normally I could tune things out, pretend they weren't there and slouch through life a carefree boyman. Noah got me thinking about the butterflies again: The time in my life when I stepped off the path and fucked things up.
All things innocent and beautiful crushed.

I had been a father for nine years when I got that text--a father but not a dad.

Noah's mother took him away before he was born. I didn't fight it; I acted upset but inside felt relieved. That probably makes me a shitty father. It was a couple of years before I saw him again. Noah was probably two or three and wearing what smelled like a full diaper.

There was my son and all I could focus on was the smell of shit.

He smiled and reached out for me. Someone was handing me a beer--I took it and thanked that person instead of acknowledging my son. I was obsessing over that memory after the text. Did he remember that day? He was probably too young to remember it but maybe he did--

Maybe it had scarred him, maybe it made him feel like he couldn't trust me.

It's funny how innocent gestures can have so many repercussions.

Innocent gestures like Noah writing "FTP" on the last school calendar I will ever print out.

# 2

The morning Noah came to live with me the trees were full
of crows. There must have been hundreds of them, maybe
even thousands. It was those birds that woke me up. The
moment my eyes opened I remembered that my son was on
his way.
Wide awake, stomach churning--what the hell had I done?
All the things my kid would need I was responsible for--
I had no idea what I was doing. None.
There wasn't even any money for a real bed so I set up my
old futon as best I could. Noah deserved better than to bed
down on Sleepy McStains.

I had been anxious the entire week between the text and
picking the Lil' Dude up at the bus stop: What do nine year
olds like to do? What do they like to eat? For me it was
video games and chicken nuggets.
I still liked chicken nuggets, maybe that would be the
bridge; maybe the two of us would bond over a big plate of
them. The crows squawked in the tree outside my window.
No, it was Grandma's ghost laughing at how stupid I am.

I pulled the covers over my head but Grandma followed me
into my sanctuary.
Closing my eyes only made it easier to see her stern face.
*You have to be a man now, no more of your nonsense.*

I could smell that my sheets needed washing. My phone beeped to remind me that it was time to get dressed and walk to the bus stop.

Leaving the house I thought about my own dad. He left one morning for work-- Who knows where the fuck he is now. One of Grandma's sayings: *The apple never falls far from the tree.*
Leave me alone, Grandma, if you love me you'll leave me alone.
That wish as I fell in with the kids walking to a new school year. All of us heading to something new, something we instinctively dreaded. Got to the bus stop, looked up and down the road, found it impossible to stand still.
*What the fuck have I gotten myself into?*
*What the fuck have I gotten* Noah *into?*
The bus came and I picked a seat near the rear doors in case I had to puke. There was an old man in a green sport jacket standing in the aisle. Green Jacket was talking to the security camera behind the driver as if it were an old friend.
I could feel the crazy coming off him like notes from an out of tune guitar.
Starting to recognize the song I made every effort to ignore him.

Followed the transit line further than I usually do. The bus took me deep into the city where people in suits ignore the homeless. Tiny brown birds were hopping along the sidewalk. Sometimes they'd stop to peck at pieces of discarded food too small for the bums to pick up. The fresh air was helping but my guts were still in a knot--would I recognize the boy? Would he recognize me?

I knew my son the second I saw him: He looked exactly as I did twenty-five years ago.

It was weird, made the whole *Dad-thing* that much more real.

I could see the recognition on Noah's face as well. There was no smile, I was just another stranger recognition or not. He looked like a serious man in miniature with his orange backpack and big, plaid suitcase. Green plaid--Cheyenne's suitcase. Maybe it had been *her* mother's but I didn't want to think about that.

"Noah?"

Still no smile; he just stood there looking at me and didn't speak for a few seconds.

"There was an old lady on the bus who reeked of piss. She looked sick like she'll be dead soon."

Where the fuck did that come from? What was I getting into?

It was too late for those sorts of questions; I grabbed his suitcase and we walked out of the station.

As I paid our bus fare Noah walked to a seat without waiting for me. I had no idea what to say or what to talk about--how do you talk to a nine year old?

The second my son sat down his phone was out. We hadn't seen each other in six years and he seemed to have no interest in me. My first response was hurt.

My second response, shortly after that, was reminding myself of all the opportunities I had to connect with Noah that I had pissed away. Choosing a cold beer over the warmth of my son was just one of them.

"You're staring--is this a thing with you?"

I wasn't sure how to respond--did we really want to get into heavy stuff so soon?

Shouldn't we keep things light for awhile before easing into deep stuff?

"Mom told me you're a musician--are you in a band?"

He was still focused on his phone but at least I could feel some of his attention.

"No."

"You seem old to be a musician."

The sound of an explosion from his phone was perfectly timed.

"People play music into their eighties."

He just shrugged and went back to whatever he was doing on his phone.

Asking him what he was doing would have felt intrusive like nosing in on a stranger's business. It made my chest hurt thinking that but that was how it was; I was a stranger to my own son. Sitting back in my seat I pretended to watch the world go by.

We got off the bus and the kid shouldered his tidy orange backpack. He paused to look at something and I tried to figure out what he was seeing. To me it was just a bunch of stacked bricks and an abandoned entrance booth.

"This used to be a gated community. No one has manned that booth for years, though."

I was talking fast and hearing the tone of desperation in my voice: Failed dad trying to engage a nine year old with facts about abandoned entrance booths. Why had I let us grow so far apart? Noah stood on his toes to look through the glass; it reminded me how small he is, a child--mine.

"I guess all these houses were expensive when they were built."

Me talking, just putting words out there. Noah looked over at me and our eyes met for the first time: His were the same color as his mother's.

"Are you rich? Mom didn't say you were but maybe you didn't tell her."

*Maybe you didn't tell her.* Even my son saw me as a fraud.

"No, I have roommates."

He shrugged and started playing the same game he had been playing on the bus.

"What's that?"

A pause long enough to make me wonder if he was even going to answer.

"Boomvest."

"Haven't heard of that one."

"You wear an explosive vest and have two minutes to get in the middle of a crowd and kill as many people as possible." For the first time I heard engagement and enthusiasm in his voice. "I got thirty-six one time."

I had no idea whether to look at it as *just a game* or if I should be worried. What would a real Dad do in a situation like that? We walked the rest of the way in a silence that was only broken by tiny explosions coming from my son's phone as he murdered innocent people.

Noah paused in the driveway and looked up at his new home.

"This place is falling apart, isn't it?"

Following his eyes, feeling too small to make words. I had stopped seeing what a wreck the place is but looking through his eyes I could see the peeling paint and weeds coming up through the driveway. Out back the grass is so high you can imagine deer grazing it.

"How many people live here?"

"Six."

He frowned, luckily it was my frown.

"Six?"

"It's a big house: Six bedrooms, three bathrooms. We call it Tatter Mansion, just don't call it that around the landlords. You probably won't see them but if you do don't call it that."

Just rambling. No thoughts, just words falling out of my mouth.

"Why wouldn't I see them?"

We were talking; I was throwing sticks at sparks trying to build something warm.

"None of us do. They never come out of the master bedroom or if they do it's when none of us are home. It's funny."

He looked up at the second floor windows and made a face. It was one of *my* faces, the second one of the day--a small victory I happily accepted. Directly over the house was a cloud shaped like a witch on a broom. It was the only cloud in the sky.

"Their room must stink." He seemed pleased by that.

"Shut-ins. Places where shut-ins live always stink."

We walked in and the house *did* smell. Noah made a face but said nothing. I realized that I didn't have a computer or anything in his room. No computer, no books, nothing to entertain him.

I was in way over my head and I'm sure he had picked up on that.

"You got a laptop or anything like that?"

He made the face Cheyenne made when I fucked something up or let her down.

"You need to borrow it?"

"No, I meant for you to watch movies and s--stuff like that."

I caught myself--swearing around him would probably be bad.

"I got one."

He went back to killing unsuspecting people in a mall. I picked up his suitcase and led him upstairs.

Noah's bedroom used to be my music room. It was going to be a home studio but I never made that happen. Shit came up and money went elsewhere.

I recorded stuff but my equipment wasn't that good. When I found out that Noah was coming I just shoved my music equipment in the closet. There wasn't enough money to make a proper room for a boy, just enough to get some sheets from Goodwill that were wrapped in plastic and covered with superheroes.

Hopefully the League of Justice would protect my son from the horrors of Sleepy McStains.

My Fender Precision knock-off bass was still on a stand. Lil' Dude went over to it and looked back at me for permission.

"Yeah, go ahead."

He played a little bit; it was impressive that his fingers were strong enough to hold down the strings. After a few seconds he put the bass back on the stand as if it were a fragile artifact.

"Are we going to eat soon, Jeff?"

Jeff, not *Dad*. That hurt in ways I hadn't expected.

"I'll make us some chicken nuggets."

He didn't look excited by that--don't kids like nuggets? I guess not.

"I have the stuff to make burritos, too."

Noah's attention went back to his phone.

"Nah, chicken nuggets are fine."

I knocked on his door thirty minutes later. The Lil' Dude was on some sort of forum page.

"What's this?"

It took my son two scanned pages of the forum before answering me.

"Boomvest forum."

Two words, may as well have been a stranger reluctantly telling me the time.

*My son hates me. The worst part is that I know I deserve it.*
Setting the plate on another part of the desk not trusting my
hands. He didn't want me there or maybe he didn't give a
shit I was there--
Either was bad; what was I supposed to do? Back off, give
him time? Try and engage him, fight to build a relationship
with my son? You get an injury and your body clenches up;
mine clenched up too tight to get words out. My guts felt
squeezed by a thousand cruel hands--they felt brittle and
then breaking apart leaving sharp edges. Old wounds, real
ones, itching under my shirt
"Enjoy your food," a weak smile was all I could manage.
He shrugged. I saw it was my shrug and that only made me
feel more overwhelmed.

In the hall I could smell the ghosts of chicken nuggets
drifting in from the kitchen. The scent of cooked breading
and over-processed meat reminded me of how clueless I
was and how I would probably fail my son. Noah was
clearly a lot smarter, a lot more insightful, and even more
cynical than myself--how could I have any authority over
him? What did I have to offer him aside from chicken
nuggets he didn't even want?
That was the beginning of the story, our story at least.

# 3

One detail, long lost, suddenly here:
Smelling Noah's sweat when I brought him the chicken nuggets that first night.
It wasn't like he was dirty or hadn't been wiping his ass, he just smelled sweaty--
Aren't nine year olds too small to be sweaty? Maybe I'm stupid but I thought kids didn't sweat until puberty.
That was the first time that I sensed that something was wrong with my son.

The smell of sweat reminded me of Gerald--
The scent of an unwashed cutting board where onions have been chopped.
I lay in bed with that realization mocking my attempts to fall asleep the night my son came to live with me. The two-fifteen sprinkler came on in the backyard muted by the tall grass. I was propped up in bed messing around with my laptop. I found and started reading all the stupid shit written when I was a teenager:
Railing against the only person who ever gave a shit, the only person who helped me.
And then Grandma died and I could do whatever I wanted.

The next morning I took Noah to register for school. They didn't want to take him and I wasn't used to fighting for him. The admissions woman had a stained purple blouse and something on her neck--

A boil, Noah told me it was a boil on the way out.
How he had seen it with his face in his game still amazes
me. Boil Woman didn't give a shit about my smile or my
excuses--
*I've heard it all so fuck off*, she may as well have said that.
In the end she did let my son in. She had this horrible smug
look on her face--I wanted to jab a pencil into the thing on
her neck just to make her scream--
Just to make her understand real cruelty and not that petty
stuff she was spooning out.
The two of us walked out and it felt like a victory. It took
me the school year to understand it wasn't.

That night I fed my son more disposable food and went to
bed. Tried to jerk off but keep seeing Gerald's face. My
videos of him were the first thing I did right, a curse
wearing the disguise of a blessing. I had been trying to get
in the viral video game for years by starting shit in Burger
King parking lots and waiting at intersections for
accidents--nothing panned out.
Grandma would have said "If at first you don't succeed try
try again."
So I did and Gerald became my star.
His cubicle was catty corner from mine at the mortgage
company. Every morning he pulled a happy voice from his
stained green backpack as he walked through the front
door. Big smile, friendly words, cold eyes. His hair was
greasy and his shirts were cheap. Get an arm's length away
and you could smell his sweat: The smell of anxiety.

Nobody knew anything about him, he was just Weird
Gerald--
Or Cheap Shirt Gerald.
Or Creepy Gerald.
One time I saw a urine stain on his pants. That was in the
second video: *Tinkle Time for Gerald.*
I got four thousand hits on that one.

# 4

The second test came when I put the first school calendar on the fridge.

It was easy to see that my son was hurting--red eyes as if they'd been leaking tears. Red eyes that were focused on the ground as if he'd been shamed.

All I could get out of him was that it has to do with bullies. Asking for more information just made him close up; I could *see* him shutting down. Did I push him for more information or give him some time? Where did I get the right to act like a Dad after nine years of absence? Grandma's voice in my head telling me not to be a pussy though not in those words.

Noah didn't still didn't want to talk but I wasn't letting him go even if the awkwardness was making my shoulders ache. He told me that the bullies had been saying shit to him; they'd been threatening him like fucking dickheads will do.

I wished that I was their age so I could fuck those bullies up and get them to leave Noah alone. When I was my son's age I never had to deal with what he was dealing with. When I was a kid I was cool: I had friends and did normal shit. No one singled me out because there wasn't anything special about me, I blended in.

Lil' Dude doesn't blend in; he's too smart to be normal.

I knew there would be problems before I sent him off to that stupid school because I'd seen the kids who went there: Little apes in trendy clothes who hooted and screeched.

I got him to talk but understood that his problems hadn't been solved. That millionth failure as a dad preoccupied me at work that next day. There had to be something I could say, right? There had to be some great advice somewhere inside me, right? When I got home from work the first thing I did was tap on his door: There was no answer. I couldn't even hear Boomvest but maybe I had tuned it out like the hum of the fridge.

What do you do when a nine year old doesn't answer their door?

*He's too young to be jerking off, right?*

I don't remember when I started but knocked a second time just to be safe. Silence on the other side of the door.

*Okay, kid, you asked for it.*

Lil' Dude was sitting on his bed playing his game with his legs crossed and a serious look on his face. He didn't even look up when I walked in.

"Hey, I knocked."

He stopped playing and looked up at me. My son's face was a mixture of hurt and anger, his expression intense enough to scare me--

It wasn't fear that he would hurt me, it was a concern becoming a certainty that he was bound to hurt others--

He was bound to hurt other people and there was nothing I could do about it.

That's how I was seeing him; a serial killer with the training wheels still on.

What kind of a parent sees their child that way?

Feeling guilty, trying to switch from seeing darkness in my boy to helping him.

*Is he okay? He doesn't look okay? Come on words, give me something motivational or at least supportive to say.*

"Uh, you doing okay?" Genius, Jeff, genius. Dad of the year for sure.

Noah shrugged but said nothing.

"School is hard for you, isn't it? Not the work, but the other kids, huh?"

Did I really want to know? What could I do to make it better if it was?

"I shouldn't let it bother me."

*Do I sit on the bed or pull a chair next to the bed? God, I suck at this.*

"Maybe not, but it still sucks." I sat on a corner of the bed. "School will be over after tomorrow and then I'll have two days to myself."

"You got any plans?"

He shrugged and picked up his phone, playing his video game as he talked.

"Do you make money as a musician?"

Redirecting the conversation back to me; his way of telling me to back off.

"No. I mean...I've made a little here and there but not enough to live off or anything."

Where did I recognize that look on his face from? Was it Gerald?

"How do you pay for things?"

No, I refused to believe that and I needed to get him back on track.

"I work in new offices, help set them up."

"I read somewhere that off gassing carpet is toxic."

"Yeah?" *Where do you come up with this shit?*

"That's what I read."

Maybe it was too soon for him to trust me with his shit. Maybe I hadn't earned his trust--no, I clearly hadn't. Noah played his game for a few seconds before talking again. There was another explosion that left a pile of what looked like intestines in the foreground.

The guts meant nothing to Noah: Maybe he was smart enough to understand it was just a fake image--

*Or maybe the thought of people being destroyed doesn't bother him.*

"How do you set them up?"

He said that as the guts disappeared and the game advanced a level.

"Take the plastic off new chairs, hook up computers, put together plastic fans--I basically take it from an empty space to a place where people can work."

A man got his arm blown off and a geyser of simulated blood spurted from the hole. I would see the look on his cartoon face in a dream several months later.

"Sounds awful."

It was but I didn't want to get negative around my son.

"At least I've got relatively steady work, not many people do these days."

"Yeah, the country is fucked."

Part of me agreed with him but part of me understood that I shouldn't encourage bad language.

*Blowing off arms and guts is okay but swear words are somehow bad?*

"Noah--that word..."

He looked up from his phone; I wasn't a hundred percent sure that the look on his face was patronizing, maybe 95 percent sure.

"This is hard for you, isn't it? Having a kid around is weird for you, I can tell."

"I guess..."

"You don't need to worry; swearing is for retards."

"I don't think we're supposed to call them that..."

"I didn't mean the mentally disabled, Jeff, I meant normal people who choose to be retards."

"Okay, well, I guess that works--"

An explosion sound came from his phone and Noah smiled a little.

I went back to my room thinking of how my son smiled playing the game. It was just a game; all the kids were playing Boomvest and they would grow up perfectly fine, right?

It was just a game but I have memories with sharp teeth. Sitting on my bed, thinking about the bloody guts--what would a real Dad do?

What would Grandma do?

My first thought was that she'd take the game away but Grandma wasn't stupid.

She would have understand that those games have social relevance--

Something the nerdy outcasts have in common with the popular kids.

With Gerald it was sports, he was always talking about the Blazers or the Ducks. I remember one time he had cornered us in the break room after a big game. G was going on about some star player but all we could see were the sweat stains under the arms of his shirt.

That would be the third video I made of Gerald: *Life is the Pits.*

*Life is the Pits* got nearly seven thousand hits.

# 5

I learned of the deer one morning when Noah left before I did.

It was my stomach, the old problems; sometimes I can't get off the toilet. By the time it was over I was running late and my son was gone. It was the first time I had unsupervised access to his room: The door was closed. I stood in the hallway making myself later. Would he have a way of telling if I went inside? Even if he did I could just say I was picking up his laundry.

Walking in all toes and tight muscles. A crow squawked outside the window.

His laptop was closed, was the computer locked? Probably; my son was very private--*is* very private. I could smell his hair and dirty clothes but his bed was made. In my head Iggy Pop was singing about bright stars in a hollow sky. He sang two verses to me as I stared at my son's laptop. My boy is smart, he probably knew how to make it so if I even *opened* his laptop he would know.

My son would know that I had violated any trust he had in me and we would be back to that moment when I saw him in the transit station.

Cue defeated Dad grabbing son's dirty clothes. Most were in a tidy pile but there was a pair of socks under his desk. His suitcase was down there, too--what if he hid stuff in there?

Another crow joined the first one; they were having some sort of bird argument.

That green plaid suitcase was judging me. It had been judging me for years, it had watched Cheyenne and I having sex. Has any man ever hated a suitcase so much? *Are you really going to snoop on Noah? What did he do to deserve this?*

I saw Gerald dancing awkwardly as Iggy Pop "la la la'd"--I *had* to look in that suitcase. The next step was making a mental note of *exactly* where it was before sliding it from under the desk. It smelled musty like there were spores in the green plaid fabric and the outside felt like skin. I put the suitcase on its side and opened it; there was nothing in there but the smell of clothes and a spiral ring notebook. The dark green cardboard still had firm corners like it had just been bought. When I kept notebooks there was always a pen was stuck in the wires--

Not Noah; another trait he hadn't picked up from me.

I realized that I had never seen Noah write with a pencil or a pen, he was always on his phone or his laptop or the pad he used for schoolwork. Could he even write? I knew a lot of kids--even smart ones--didn't have the ability.

Opening the notebook I saw that there was only one paragraph written in it:

*I was thinking about the first time I saw a deer.*
*Not in a video or a picture--in real life.*
*That's a wild animal not a pet; that's what I thought.*
*It came right up because I had been checking out a knot in a tree.*
*I looked over at it and it looked back at me.*
*Hearing a crack behind me I waved my arms.*
*The deer ran off and there was trouble for me.*

The Passenger gave way to Baker Street. Noah had bad handwriting, barely legible. Block letters, all caps-- Standing there, making myself even more later; trying to make sense of what my kid had written. I could ask my son but he would have been pissed off that I had gone in his suitcase.

No, he would be worse than pissed off.

Ask his mother? Yeah, I knew how that would go.

Cue defeated dad putting the notebook back in the suitcase and sliding suitcase back under the desk.

# 6

The second calendar had cartoon witches on orange paper for Halloween. One was flying a broom in front of a black circle moon. The other was putting a stick in what looked like a big pot. That was an uneasy thirty-one days with those witches in the corner of my eye as I cooked meals or made coffee.

*The deer ran off and there was trouble for me.*
Idaho. Even a dummy like me understood that it was about Idaho. Okay, but *what*? Was someone scaring the deer off when they approached my son? Was the "trouble" some sort of sexual molestation? Had Cheyenne sent him away to keep him safe? As much as I didn't want to see her as the better parent I really didn't want to think of Noah dealing with that sort of thing.
It *would* explain why he was so guarded and solemn, though.

Even if we left at the same time Noah wasn't really walking with me, he was off in his own Noah-bubble playing his game. There was a dog next door that challenged the fence and barked when my boy passed. Lil' Dude definitely did not like that. I remember the way he would scowl into his phone. The only time his face came out of his phone was to check out the crows in the trees. He wanted to leave out bread for them and I had to be the bad guy: My argument was that human food is bad for animals but he outsmarted me by pointing out that they ate discarded food all the time. All I could do was throw up my hands and start buying stale bread for my son's new friends--his only friends.

Noah was smarter and more insightful than me but I still learned things:
He thought baths were disgusting and only took showers.
He did not like nuggets and preferred healthier food. Processed shit clearly wouldn't cut it; part of becoming a *real dad* would involve making grown-up food. I had never cooked much, fajitas and fried potatoes taxed my culinary skill. My son made me aware of green stuff that we were supposed to be eating--a nine year old telling his parents he wanted vegetables. Completely lost, I went online and got some recipes. I'd make lists of proteins and legumes and green things that I'd go over as I rode the bus to the grocery store. The part of the store with fruits and vegetables may as well have been an unknown city and I pushed the cart in unsure circles as I tried to find fresh broccoli and raw black beans. Everything looked inedible and clearly lacked breading or a healthy layer of cheese. Punishment in food form, penance for the years of being a bad father.

Standing in line for the self-checkout I got to thinking about the notebook. Why had I opened that fucking suitcase? All I had achieved was revealing another mystery about my son that I would probably never solve. Had I smoothed the tracks after sliding it back under the desk?

Or, had Noah seen them and whatever trust he had in me turned to dust and drifted out the open door?

Once again I was where I didn't belong crushing things fragile and innocent.

Two teens were watching an episode of *Folkz Die* at the bus stop. A motorcyclist was cut in half by a distracted driver and it was giving them the giggles. When Noah was born those shows were nearly unknown:

*Folkz Die. Life Hurtz.*

It was fringe shit you had to search for--I remember because I was trying to get in that game. Paid a bum $20 one time to yell a racial slur in a BK parking lot. Gave another one $15 to roll her cart into traffic. I filmed everything with my phone but nothing panned out until Gerald and the nine videos he starred in.

Putting the groceries away I saw that someone had written "We're here" next to the cartoon witch on the school calendar.

*We're here*--Tatter Mansion is not a good place to think about that sort of shit.

If you thought it was too new to be haunted you'd be wrong. Noah coming into my life had reminded me of the ghosts that surround us.

In that house, in the world.

There was some mummified celery in a brown puddle in the vegetable bin. I thought about cleaning it but realized that I wasn't ready for that degree of maturity. Tyler walked in as I closed the fridge. He was wearing his sweatpants without drawers and you could see his dick: Someone may as well have written "we're here" on the fabric next to his cock and balls. In the past it was whatever but now that Noah was around--

Part of me was thinking "He's going to be a man someday" and all that but it was still gross.

And now I was staring and Tyler could see I was staring.

"What's poppin', bro?"

A smile somehow formed on my face. Does anyone still say what's poppin'?

I wasn't ready for the dick talk. Maybe I could start with something more innocuous.

"Hey, I need to do a big shopping trip and was wondering if I could borrow your car. Anytime that works, bro."

He made a face. I was trying not to stare at the outline of his dick but I already had and was pretty sure that he had caught me. Tyler wants to get a penis implant and I don't get it; thing already looks big. Maybe it's like women and tits, insecurity or something. Who knew; I just wanted my roommate to start wearing underwear.

"Sorry, bro, the car I'm using now is really expensive; if I get caught it could be my ass."

I was focusing on the sink, a neutral area that wasn't his junk.

"No worries."

Standing there, getting angry at Noah for forcing me to be a dad and talk to other dudes about their lack of underwear.

"Hey, you didn't tell me what you think!" Tyler leaned forward to show me his scalp. "New plugs are coming in."

"Hey, yeah, looks good!"

It looked like a drunk chimp had glued black toothbrush heads on his scalp.

"Cheaper than the dick surgery, bro. Man, I'll be saving another year or two for that."

I had been dealing with *The Unfolding Tale of Brax Shlong* for nearly a year.

Tyler sold new cars and hated it. He made good money but couldn't stand his job. My roommate was always telling me about *how stupid people are* and the tricks he used on the lot to get people to buy some shitty car or other. Instead of renting a decent apartment Tyler saved that money for the plugs, the bigger dick, and a personal trainer.

The goal was to be a porn star named Brax Schlong.

I got all this on the first day we met--*first fucking day*. *Think about it, bro, it's the best job in the world: You get paid for fucking as many chicks as you want.*

It seemed like a stupid idea to me--isn't porn free in the age of the internet?

You'd think that but obviously it's a thing. There are even motivational videos by some guy named Biff Harder. I've seen the videos; Tyler made the roommates sit through a couple of them.

That was the most awkward hour of my life.

"You okay, bro?"

"Yeah--"

"You just looked as if you had a stroke for a minute, there."

"Just tired, I guess. New at this dad thing."

He smiled a little but I could tell he didn't give a shit. It was probably the same smile he used to put people into a new Kia and out of a debt-free life.

"How is the little man doing?"

"Great." The answer I knew I was supposed to give.

"Cool beans." Tyler grabbed some chips and went back to his room.

My roommate is a part of the story, a reminder of what happens when you step off the path and crush a butterfly. If I had stayed on the path he probably would have settled into selling Kias with the goal of becoming a manager or something. He would have met some girl at Chili's and they would have gotten married and bought a condo together where he wore underwear and didn't ask "What's poppin'."

A boring solid life.

Those kids at the bus stop would be holding doors open for old ladies and planning for careers in middle management. I can't help but feel I'm responsible, that I created this world.

We went through the days of the calendar of the witch. I learned to make lentils and greens and other responsible adult foods. When I wasn't making inedible breading-free food there was the struggle to come up with Good Dad advice and try to be there for my son. Part of me wanted none of it and resented all the green stuff we had to eat and the efforts I had to make--the continuing war between the new Jeff and the boyman I still was. Did I check out the new brewpub? No, I had to save money to buy a real bed and send Sleepy McStains away. More Good Dad words came to me and I believe the love I have for my son came through--

Then there would be the retreat to my room where everything I bottled up could be freed. That carefree boyman slouching through life refused to die. He resented Noah and all the responsibilities my son brought in his tidy orange backpack.

I locked that side of myself in the closet but he was moaning through the door.

Life had become so complicated, so real.

The boyman escaped the closet a couple of times and grabbed my phone. He started to text Cheyenne to see if her mother could take Noah after all. Each time I wrestled the phone away I wondered if I was being a genuinely good guy or if it was just fear of adding more ghosts in my life.

The boyman pointed out more things about Noah--not just his obsession with Boomvest, loads of kids were into that game. Not just how solitary he was, I've heard more kids are keeping to themselves.

It was the flashes of intense anger that came up for no reason.

Shaking heat crackling off him that made me step back.

His hair, how he let it get greasy like Gerald's.

The smell of his hair took me back to that office, back in the caterpillar days when I mounted a GoPro in a fake plant to capture Gerald's routines. It caught his real face, the one we all saw on the last day. The face my son would make years later as he waved. Gerald's real face would not be seen by my viewers until the ninth video.

# 7

Near the end of the witch days I had to go to Noah's
school. They wouldn't say what the problem was over the
phone so I took half a day off work that I couldn't afford.
The halls were full of kids when I went to the school office.
The air was nearly slick with giddy perfumes and body
sprays. Part of me wanted to see Noah but part of me
dreaded it--how was I supposed to act if I ran into him? My
Grandma embarrassed the shit out of me in school; she'd
yoo-hoo and wave and clearly didn't give a fuck how much
I was embarrassed. Not waving back would earn me a strict
talking to the next time I was trapped in the car with her.
I was determined not to make my son feel that sort of
humiliation.
But what then? Ignore him?
Boyman leaning against lockers, shaking his head--
*Didn't feel this sort of anxiety two months ago.*
Never ran into Lil' Dude which was probably for the best.
Part of me was curious to see what he was like at school.
Part of me understood that he was probably anxious and
uncomfortable; seeing that would have sucked.

There were security cameras everywhere. Some were
subtle, some not. It made me think of GoPros hidden in
plants like the one I had hidden in Gerald's cubicle and a
smaller one I had tucked away in another part of our
offices. There was definitely trouble for me related to that

second camera, a story I'm still working on coming to terms with.

They had me cool my heels in the lobby with several other bored looking parents. It smelled like disinfectant and somebody wearing too much perfume: Not giddy perfume, chained down in adulthood perfume. All the magazines were ancient homemaking and cooking ones, not that any of us took our noses out of our phones. My name came out of a fucked up speaker like a gollum clearing its throat. I walked down the lobby to a door with the faded number that had followed my name. The room was the size of a walk-in closet with three chairs. The woman with the boil from when I had registered Noah was sitting in one of them. She looked like she was holding in a fart and reeked of baby powder and cigarettes. I think the boil had gotten bigger. Small talk lasted for as long as it took me to close the door and pick a chair.
"We have our concerns about Nathan."
"Nathan?"
"Your son?"
"Noah."
"Yes, sorry. Noah. We have our concerns about Noah."
The memory of wanting to pop her boil with a pencil returned. The counselor had horrible person coming out of her pores--that and dead cigarettes.
"You are aware we run biometrics in all our classes--"
"No--biometrics?"

Neck Boil scrolled through some pages on the pad resting on her lap. For one horrifying moment I imagined her without pants, baby powder dusting a huge bush.

"You signed the form authorizing it, I can show you--"

"No, that's okay; what is going on with Noah?"

"His biometrics show anger and frustration. He also texts a lot of questions to the teacher."

*He's way too smart for your dipshit teachers, case closed.*

"Is that a bad thing? I thought kids were supposed to ask questions."

She looked up at me as if she knew that I knew about the baby powder in her enormous pubic beard.

"We're more concerned with the data from the biometrics. If Noah is going to remain enrolled at this school we need to at least get him *close* to the required parameters."

Baker Street was back in my head, the sax riff on a loop.

"Required parameters?"

"I can send you the information about the normal ranges and Noah's readings. Our records show that Noah is not on any medication, no Prozac or Ritalin or Selfaway."

"No…"

Neck Boil looked up with the sort of smile that almost makes slapping another human being acceptable.

"Maybe you should take him to a doctor, see what a professional thinks."

A smile somehow formed on my face; the sax solo cut to the ferocious guitar solo.

"Yeah."

"One last thing and this isn't a school requirement more something you should be aware of: Noah's web activity…"

"You mean the Boomvest forum? Yeah, I know he spends a lot of time on that--"

"We're not worried about that, Boomvest is just a game. Your son has started looking into things like 9-11 conspiracies, the writings of Noam Chomsky, things like that. He needs to be aware that when applying for colleges and jobs in the future his search histories could come back to haunt him."

"I'll talk to him." No, I won't.

Another smile that didn't come within a hundred miles of her eyes.

"Thank you, and I'll send you that information about biometrics. Ask your doctor about Selfaway, it really has helped a lot of kids."

# 8

The calendar for November had a turkey and a man with a stick. I asked Noah why there was a man with a stick and he rolled his eyes.

His "I'm smarter than you" face was probably one of the reasons why kids picked on him.

"See that thing on his head, Jeff? That's a pilgrim's hat."

"Yeah?" It was coming back to me, all that shit they taught us as kids. "The stick is a rifle, right?"

"They called them muskets back then, single shot rifles. Took a long time to reload."

Something about him talking about *shots* and *reloading* made me uncomfortable. Boyman was nudging me, suggesting I call Cheyenne's mother--

I pushed him away--I wouldn't give up...as much as I was tempted to.

The complex food I made for my son perplexed my guts. Noah started complaining about the smells I created in the bathroom. Was it time to tell him why my digestive system doesn't work right? Was he old enough to handle that story?

It didn't matter, *I* wasn't ready.

Twelve years and the anxiety built to a scream if I even thought about it--

A peek, just one eye around a corner was all I could handle. Noah would have lots of questions and I would have to stand in the full light of my memories.

I started hovering outside Noah's door--

World's Worst Dad, they should make *that* cup.

I'd hover and pace knowing that I had to find words and say them to him--

Words, like a cat, watching me from an unreachable distance.

Maybe it didn't matter; my son never really seemed to care about whatever came out of my mouth. Every time I stepped in his room he was either playing Boomvest or scrolling the game's forum or watching violent videos. He may not have noticed me but I noticed changes in his life.

I remember this one day after school, there was a lot of light coming through the window for November. Looking over his shoulder, noticing that Boomvest was different somehow.

"It looks like there's a second guy on there with you."

He kept playing--was he even going to answer? Had he heard me? Did I need to repeat the question or would that have been playing *his* game? Noticing the way the monitor lit his face I wondered if that was how Gerald looked when he was ten--a bullied loner with greasy hair who spent too much time on the computer.

"When you get to the eighteenth level you get a second guy."

"Second guy?"

Could he hear the desperation in my voice? Boyman grabbed my collar and pulled me back so I wasn't breathing down Noah's neck. Inside I was still a hopeless father clawing at his son, trying to get *anything* from him.

"Makes it easier to get more kills."

"So...you have two guys with vests you control?"

"Kinda, but he has free will so you have to bribe him."

Noah paused the game to turn around and explain things to me as I tried to look normal and not like I was excited that he had paused the game to talk to me.

"It's part of what makes the game trickier. You have a second suicide bomber and if you space him or her right you get a lot more kills. The problem is that Bubb has a mind of his own."

"Bubb--you mean the second guy with the vest?"

"Yeah."

"So...how do you get him to do what you want?"

Noah turned back around and unpaused the game.

"Promised him that I'd give five goats to his family. He wouldn't go along with my plan until he got a text saying the goats had arrived."

Two big explosions. One of Bubb's hands landed on the escalator and rode it up.

"It looks like the hand is waving."

"Yeah, the graphics of this game are pretty swell."

I sat on the edge of Sleepy McStains trying to come up with ways to keep the conversation going. There was an old stain on the futon--vomit:

A party four years ago. Cute girl I was trying to hook up with. She was hanging off me and there was hope but she got too drunk and puked on the corner of Sleepy McStains.

All I got from that chick was a vomit stain the shape of New Zealand.

If I started getting skill at Boomvest would my son respect me?

Would I suddenly become someone he paid attention to and wanted to hang out with?

Or, would it be like my friendliness with the girl who left the New Zealand stain: Not real. Ulterior motivations. Temporary until the mood passed.

I was sitting a few feet away from him trying to turn miles into yards into feet.

"How far does this game go, Noah?"

His hand hovered over his phone; I had never noticed how stubby and fat my son's fingers were.

"No one knows. There's this girl who has gotten up to the forty-first level. Everyone thought forty was it but then she got to another level. She says it gets harder to control your accomplices and they betray you and stuff."

The cat with the words was curled on my lap but I could see by the twitching of its tail that it was preparing to run.

"You think you'll ever get tired of it?"

His face soured and he shook his head, feet became yards again--

An innocent question I was made to feel guilty for asking. I could smell his hair, smell his sweat; I was an intruder in his lair.

There was a door, though, a big golden door--

What was on the other side? What was *really* on the other side? Whatever it was, I understood that it wasn't real.

"Try to get to sleep by ten, okay?"

Noah said nothing, I hadn't expected him to. Cue defeated dad leaving his boy's room.

Grandma wouldn't have slunk out like a shamed dog. She would have shut that computer down and been in Noah's face.
I know this because it happened:
Cue old lady confronting rude teen with a barrage of words--
Where did she find those words? Where did she get the courage to use them? Where did she find the hope those words would pay off?
Love--that was probably the answer to each question.
Maybe I never loved Noah. It's a horrible thought but maybe that's why I couldn't do it. I look back at what Grandma did and see that she loved me.
I look back at those early days with Noah and question my love for him. Did I tell myself I loved him because a Good Dad would love his son? I keep seeing my boy waving and the way it breaks my heart has to be love, right?
And then I look at all the times I accepted his rejection and walked out of his room--didn't try to fight, didn't put in the effort to build our bond.
Cue tortured dad opening another beer and feeling like he failed his son.

# 9

I am remembering another night a couple of days before
we got to the end of the turkey and man with stick
calendar--
Noah heard the laughter all of us have heard in the Tatter
Mansion. There was a storm right before Thanksgiving, the
first big one of the season. Vicious rain and wind with
crazed laughter mixed in that sounded like it was coming
from another part of the house. In the middle of all that
there was a nervous tapping on my door that almost caused
me to piss myself.
"Yeah?"
My son pushed the door open, he was scared but struggling
not to show it.
"What the fuck is up with this house, Jeff?"
Deciding not to punish him for swearing I patted the side of
the bed optimistically; he stuck a pin in that balloon by
remaining just inside the door. The laughter again--Noah
quickly closed the door but kept his distance from me.
"What is that?" Wanting to give into his fear, wanting to
seek comfort, but--
Cue memory of a baby reaching out for a man who'd rather
cradle a beer.
"I don't know."
"Isn't this place too new to be haunted?"
Boyman was on my shoulder breathing in my ear. He
suggested that I tell Noah the house was built on an Indian
burial ground so my boy would beg to go live with Gail.

"I don't know--"

"Don't you know anything?!"

Anger, genuine anger--how did so much rage fit in such a small body? I just sat in my bed with my hands squeezing the hem of my quilt. Was the hurt that I felt because I loved him? Only people you love can hurt you like that, right?

"Noah, you have every right to be angry with me..."

The words left me after sending ten soldiers to fight a battle that needed ten thousand. It was over in a second, I had thrown kerosene on a fire. Noah walked out of my room--I had vanquished his fear with my failure as a dad.

# 10

Went into Noah's room again. The League of Justice has
been stripped off Sleepy McStains and badly folded in the
closet. I just stood there looking at the bed, fixating on the
stain the shape of New Zealand--

Did he see New Zealand? Probably not; he would probably
see something smart like an amoeba or something. I look at
New Zealand and remember that the girl didn't go away:
She spent the night on Sleepy McStains and we had
breakfast the next morning. New Zealand girl drove us to a
restaurant I can't recall the name of. I remember she was
playing really bad pop music and her car smelled like gym
clothes. New Zealand girl was pretty, though, and I was
reaching into my bag of hook up tricks through a hangover.
We got on well enough at that restaurant that there was a
second date--

YepperDeppers, that's where we went. She had a colorful
drink and I found myself staring at her neck and wondered
what it would be like to kiss it. After the color was drained
from her glass New Zealand girl came back to the Tatter
Mansion--

First, we kissed in her car; I can remember the taste of fried
shrimp and rum.

Things were going well, it felt like we were going to hook
up. We went up to my room. I put my hand on the outside
of her shirt and cupped a breast. NZ girl looked down shyly
and laughed a little.

"I want to look at stuff with you, okay?"

"Yeah." Getting up to grab my laptop, stopped by a curious look on her face.

"Where are you going?"

"I thought you wanted to look at stuff?"

A smile, a beautiful smile I still see when I really hate myself.

"I have things, come back here."

New Zealand girl crawled to the end of the bed and grabbed her bag. After a few seconds of rummaging she pulled out a couple of magazines: *Dangerous Dongs* and *Studz*. My first reaction was surprise: I didn't know people still bought porn magazines. My second reaction--

My second reaction is the reason this is still a story, one of *my* stories.

Something about those magazines bothered me…

Something about them made me so anxious that I thought I was going to puke. NZ girl was watching my face.

"Is everything okay?"

Why do people ask that when it's clear things definitely aren't okay?

"Yeah, sure." Why do we feel the need to lie?

"You got a problem with these?"

She held up one of the magazines. The guy on the cover was ripped and you could see a huge bulge in the front of his jeans. I *did* have a problem with them--

This war came out of nowhere: I wanted to fuck New Zealand girl but I'm guessing her kink was looking at those magazines and I really didn't want to look at them.

*Come on, it's just a bunch of naked bros fooling around with other naked bros--you've seen guys with big dicks fooling around with other guys with big dicks before.*

On line. Why was it okay online but her magazines were freaking me out?

"Do you need those to....uh, have sex?"

Those words, not thinking, just scrambling to keep things progressing through the need to puke. Her face went from curious to realizing something she didn't like.

"You're a dick."

New Zealand girl, now clearly pissed off and putting the magazines back in her bag. I could see her nipples through her shirt and was getting an erection and it just made more of a mess of the whole situation.

I had no response to *you're a dick,* I was still having what must have been a panic attack even after she shoved the magazines back in her bag. Looking back I wonder why she was so angry, why she hadn't been more flexible--

More pointless questions I like to poke myself with when dwelling on all the missed opportunities in my life.

New Zealand girl jumped off my bed with her bag over her shoulder and ran out of my room. I heard her stomp down the stairs and slam the front door of the Tatter Mansion. I sat in the middle of my bed with an erection trying to figure out what the fuck had happened. I had never thought that I had a problem with gay guys but maybe I could never admit that, maybe it took a cute girl with her old school magazines to bring it out.

Maybe seeing that guy's huge dick through his jeans made me feel things I have never been able to face.

In that moment with her cheap perfume still on my clothes
I had no idea.

# 11

December's calendar had a cartoon Santa on it.

Noah needed a new coat and I had to make a choice: New jacket or new bed. In the beginning he had complained about the way Sleepy McStains smelled but the complaints stopped. Had he gotten used to it? No. He was just bottling his anger up--

Bottling things up just like Gerald did--same greasy hair, same habit of bottling shit up.

We had a fight on Thanksgiving Day. I went through all this work to make us a decent meal and Noah kept making faces and picking at his food. I asked him what was up and he said my cooking sucked. Sucked. Boyman was smirking at me from one of the unoccupied chairs.

*See, this is the way it's going to be as long as the brat is here; whatever you do will never be good enough.*

The kid let me have it about my cooking and Sleepy McStains and how I was a dumbshit. He didn't put it that way but his intention was clear. I was already feeling guilty about him needing a new coat; he never said anything but I saw him hugging himself when it started to get cold. My son probably didn't speak up because he knew I'd just get him some halfass coat from Goodwill or something.

Well, it was either that or him enduring the continuing saga of Sleepy McStains.

I explained as much the day I put the Santa calendar up.

"Why did you even bring me here if you can't buy the stuff I need, Jeff?"

Noah reminded me so much of his mother I wanted to slap him.

"Bro, they were going to send you to live with your grandmother. Do you want that?"

I caught Boyman kneeling in prayer over by the window and flipped him off.

"Your mother?"

"No, Gail."

"What about your mother?"

"I have no fucking idea where she is!" Had I yelled at my son?

Another father of the year award was waiting for me. Noah didn't seemed scared or angry, he looked as if he pitied me which just made everything worse--

I was such a fucking mess my ten year old kid felt sorry for me.

"I can live with the bed, maybe Febreeze it or something. Used jackets are creepy, though, you never know how much used tissues have been in the pockets."

"You mean from people blowing their noses?"

He turned back to his phone.

"Or jerking off."

Was it normal for a kid so young to know about jerking off? Did I need to have some sex talk with him? I had been hoping I'd be spared that shit for at least another year or two.

"You know what I wonder, Jeff?"

*Please don't let it be about jerking off or where babies come from or what a blumpkin is.*

"What?"

"Have you heard of the Golden Bullet board?"

*Okay, this is even worse.*

"Those freaks obsessed with getting shot at work? Yeah."

Was I about to throw up? It was a possibility.

"Where did it start? Do you know?"

I saw on the tab bar that he had been watching the last Gerald video--

What did my son think and feel when he saw those people being shot? Did he like it? Did it disgust him but he still felt compelled to watch it?

*Did he think that the shooter was missing opportunities?*

Fuck you, Boyman.

"I don't know, I first heard of it a few years ago. They're idiots, Noah, you can't make someone go crazy and shoot up an office."

He switched tabs so the Gerald video was up on the screen; a still of Gerald smiling his terrible smile.

*You can't make someone go crazy and shoot up an office.*

Or can you?

*A Sound of Thunder*, that was the name of the Butterfly story--

I don't remember the writer's name except it sounds like a candy bar.

"On the Golden Bullet Board they have dozens of discussions about these Gerald videos, like this is what caused the Board to be started."

I didn't want to be a Dad anymore, not if it meant having to talk about that sort of shit.

"Don't know, never heard that."

That seemed to satisfy my son. He asked if we could shop for new coats the following day and then started a new round of Boomvest and I ceased to exist.

Gerald had a thing for this chick named Anna. She was skinny, not much in the way of tits, pretty face. Intelligent but in a sarcastic way I didn't dig. Everyday he went out of his way to talk to her--everyday. Gerald was so awkward it made me cringe--
Didn't stop me from filming it.
He cornered Anna in the break room one morning. She was trying not to act freaked out but you could tell she was by her body language--
Going rigid, clenching and unclenching the fingers on her left hand.
Gerald had an erection, a small crooked one like a secret stick. I wanted to call the video *Gerald Gets a Secret Stick* but for some reason YouTube wouldn't allow it.
Instead I settled for calling the fourth video *Gerald Tries to Get a Date*.
That video got more than 21,000 hits.
Remembering that video brings back more memories--
A couple of weeks after I made that video Anna and I were chatting in the breakroom. We got along. Not in a potential to date way but we got along.
She was laughing at something I said--probably something about Gerald--and touched me on the arm. It was at that moment that Gerald walked in. He saw the love of his life touching my arm and the face he made…

Fifteen plus years later it still scares me, makes me wish I could get hypnotized to lose the memory or something. Gerald looked like he wanted to kill both of us, you could see it and *feel* it.

And then he tried to cover it up with this horrible fake smile before busting into Prince's "I Wanna Be Your Lover."

His falsetto wasn't bad but the gyrations that went with it were.

"Ooops, I'll give you guys the room!"

He laughed a little too brightly and walked out of the breakroom. Anna and I just looked at each other.

"What the fuck was that?"

I had no answer then but a shrug.

If you asked me today my answer would have been "Our fate."


Cut to: Me walking home from the bus stop after work. A Kia pulling up to the curb and honking--Tyler. It was raining but he had let me walk in the rain before.

After dropping in the passenger seat and closing the door I was surrounded by his loud cologne and whatever bro country rap he was listening to.

"Couldn't let you walk in the rain, bro."

I laughed and thanked him but knew something was up. Tyler turned down the music.

"Hey, I need to talk to you about the little man."

I still hadn't talked to him about his lack of underwear and now he had an ace over me regarding my son.

"What about him?"

"Bro...this is totally awkward for reals but your kid gave me this hard look the other day. It was a total shooting spree face."

"Shooting spree face? What did you say to him?"

"Nothing, I said nothing bad, I just told him maybe you wouldn't like him drawing a dick on Santa."

"A dick. On Santa?"

"Yeah, I didn't mean to overstep on your shit or anything, I just felt I had to say something."

My son defacing his school calendar with a St. Nick prick had brought out Tyler's parental instincts?

And Noah had responded with a *shooting spree* face?

"Did he say anything?"

Tyler realized we were passing the driveway and hard braked.

"Shit, sorry bro. Uh, no, he just stepped back, stared at me, then all stomped off."

"I'll talk to him."

"Cool, I mean, I don't want there to be any bad shit between us. Like I said, I didn't mean to come at him like I was his dad or anything."

"No, I get it."

*Please stop talking. I can see your penis on your leg through your slacks. Do you ever wear underwear?*

I never talked to Noah about the shooting spree face just as I never suggested to Tyler that he start wearing underwear. Grandma would have talked to me if I made some hard ass face. We had some little wiggas on our street making pathetic attempts to act *gangsta*. Grandma pointed them out to me and then playfully grabbed my ear.

"If I see you acting like that I do this but I twist, I *twist*." She did it a little but laughed to let me know she was playing. I told her to let go. *I hate you, you mean old bitch.* Twenty years later I am still angry that I even thought that. Grandma loved me enough to get in my face and keep me from becoming a shit. She gave me rules, shoved me off, and instructed me to stay on the path. When she died the first thing I did was step off that fucking path.

And the rest is history.

# 12

The Santa schlong was in pencil and easily erased. Mr. Claus lost his dick but a couple of days later gained a word balloon: *Nothing for you.*
Nothing for you--what the fuck did that mean? Who had written it? Noah? It didn't look like his handwriting but he was clever enough to disguise it.
Should I have asked him if he wrote it and if so why?
No, I understood why: He thought I wouldn't get him a Christmas present. Or, if I got him one, some piece of shit from Goodwill.
But I still had to talk to him about it, right?
This was some passive-aggressive way of lashing out, right?
*Before he gets a gun in a few years and really lashes out.*
Fuck you, Boyman.
Must have paced the kitchen looking over my shoulder at that calendar for ten minutes. I was already thinking about Idaho--
*The deer ran off and there was trouble for me.*
What had gotten him kicked out of that commune? Was it bratty stuff, bitching about food and rules? Or, he had done something *really* bad, something violent?
Did the deer run off because he was fucking around with a rifle or something?

By the month of the Santa calendar I had Noah taking a gun and shooting things up. Everytime I told myself that

was stupid I remembered the time he talked about rifles and the time it took to reload them--
Noah seemed to know what he was talking about.
And there was his interest in the Golden Bullet forum. What if he was planning something like that? What if he was trying to drive another kid to shoot up the school? He said the people on that forum were idiots but he could have just been trying to throw me off.
In the kitchen, pacing, the sensation of being watched creating cold spots on my back.
As the days grew darker the house became more...ominous: The laughter. The footsteps. The shadows in weird places. How was I supposed to raise a sane child in a place like that?

Grandma never beat me. The closest she got to that was twisting my ear when she pointed out the wigga kids in the neighborhood. A beating wasn't her style, plus she was small and not very strong looking. Grandma didn't need to raise a hand, though, the faces she made scared me enough. She was especially strict around Christmas--
At the time it pissed me off because I was already dealing with a lot of shit. I'd be thinking about Mom or Dad, dwelling on them like an idiot. It hurt, obviously; I wasn't old enough to understand what dicks they were, I just missed them.
And Grandma would be in my face about my grades or cleaning the kitchen.
I told her that she was mean; that was as rebellious as I dared get to her face. There were times when I fucking

hated that old lady, it's only now that I think I get it. She loved me. She was hurting, too, she was hurting because she could see that I was hurting. Maybe she felt like a bad parent because she had raised a child that had ended up a shitty parent. Maybe Grandma didn't know how to comfort me or maybe she was so pissed off at my parents that it had short circuited her gentle and loving side. I'd always get one amazing present at Christmas: One. Grandma didn't have much money.

And I'd bitch to my buddies about Cheap Ass One Gift Grandma.

I didn't know how good I had it.

# 13

January's calendar had a baby on it--Baby New Year, I guess. It reminded me of the time I chose a beer over Noah--what if he saw it and was reminded of when I ignored him? I printed it at work and debated whether or not I should bring it home.

Would it fuck up all the bonding shit I had been working on with my son?

Would it bring back that afternoon vividly, remind Noah why he didn't trust me?

If it did he never said anything. I put it on the fridge, saw him look at that stupid baby cartoon, but he never said anything. My son kept things to himself but I had learned his faces by then--

I never saw him look troubled like he was reliving a bad memory when he looked at that baby picture.

It was still a fucking relief when I got to take that calendar down.

Noah got a new coat, a nice green one. He seemed to really like it and that was something I had never felt before--

I wasn't aware doing something for someone else could feel so good.

There are times I go in his closet and look at that coat. Sometimes I just open the door and look but others I will touch the sleeve or something--

It's stupid, I know.

Noah liked his new coat and acted all happy and shit--he seemed like a normal, happy kid.

Maybe all his weirdness was just a phase and by the time he got to middle school he wouldn't be such an outcast.

I was thinking that the morning I sent Noah off to school in his new coat.

And then there was some excitement next door: The neighbors' mutt had died.

No, the neighbors' dog had been *brutally murdered*.

Hearing excited voices next door I went to the window and saw four bros somewhere in their late twenties standing around a dead dog.

"Look, look right here, bro--"

"A wild animal could have done that."

"No way, those are slash marks from a knife."

Realizing that if they looked up and saw me they'd probably come over and kick my ass I backed away from the window and went back to getting ready for work.

*No way, those are slash marks from a knife.*

First thought: Worry; my son walking the same streets as a violent killer.

Second thought. Maybe...no, not even going there.

But I had to.

With one sock on I went down to the kitchen and rummaged through the drawers. Over the years tenants had left behind bowls and silverware and cooking knives. There were three of them: A skinny one I think is a filet knife. One the size of a butter knife but sharp as hell. A big one for chopping--or slashing.

That last one was missing when I checked the drawer.

It wasn't in the drawer, it wasn't on the counter, and it wasn't in the sink.

*Come on, Jeff. There has to be an explanation.*

But what was it? Tyler using it to turn his never worn underwear into shoe polishing rags? I thought of my son and then the seventh Gerald video I made.

Hearing laughter from another part of the house I understood that it was time to go.

Walking to the bus stop I did a search: *I Think Gerald Kills Pets*. Ghost of past pain drifting through my gut, the sound of crunching. The seventh Gerald video had gotten 28,000 hits by that point. I found it as I climbed on the bus and fumbled for my pass with my free hand. Green Jacket was on the bus having a friendly chat with the camera behind the driver. I took a seat next to a fat man in a musty smelling coat.

"Bro, I seen that. Guy with the greasy hair totally killed those dogs."

A teenager was looking over my shoulder: Dirty clothes. Bored Voice. I paused the video and looked over my shoulder at him.

"Yeah?"

"The way he talks about that shit; it's creepy as fuck."

Another teenager elbowed him and mumbled. Both young men looked up at the man in the green jacket. Laughing, they walked up towards the front of the bus.

Were they going to mess with him? What the fuck was I going to do if they did?

The kid who had been talking to me was reaching in his pocket--

What was in there? A pen to write on the green jacket? A knife? I really didn't want to get in the middle of that shit--how was it my business? I already had a kid to take care of--

*And this is the world he has to spend the next seventy or eighty years in.*

Starting to get up, seeing the kid was pulling out some cigarettes, sitting back down. Boyman reminded me how Noah caused all the stress in our lives.

The video paused on a shot of the right side of Gerald's face as he smiled one of his gruesome smiles.

A programmed smile on the face of a robot that doesn't understand emotions.

A robot with a virus in its software:

*The way he talks about that shit; it's creepy as fuck.*

Yes it was.

Gerald cornered three of us in the breakroom. I always pretended to be going over texts but the camera was on.

Part of me thinks G knew he was being filmed--

The nods he gave me from time to time.

He gave seven of those nods the day we shot *I think Gerald Kills Pets*.

Laughing as he tells the story of a dog in his neighborhood--a neighbor's mutt; he didn't like the neighbor. Neighbor was a buff guy with a fancy truck who called Gerald a fag one time.

"A *fag*!" Gerald laughed, looking at Anna's tits.

The dog would bark at Gerald whenever he walked by, Gerald didn't like that.

He laughed as he told the story but his eyes had narrowed and one of his hands was shaking a little. There was dirt under his nails as if he had been burying something. I switched off the video but could still hear his laugh and smell his greasy hair. What if Noah had taken the knife? Taking a breath, preparing myself for the next part.

*What if...no, not going there.*

No. I couldn't; not unless there was evidence. Hard evidence.

Until then I was putting the thought out of my head.

# 14

I never found the chopping knife in Noah's room.

# 15

The dead dog lay below my window for a week. Crows came by the peck at it and I imagine other things were coming up from the ground and burrowing into it. The next door bros had discovered it at the beginning of a school week, when the week ended a small white van showed up in front of their house. I made myself late for work by watching the city worker pick the carcass up. He or she was in khaki with a green cap that had the City's logo on it. A bro in sweat pants and an electric green tank top let them in the side gate and followed them to where the dog was. The city worker laid out what looked like a body bag next to the body. I wondered what sort of life that dog had--was it a loved pet or mostly just left by itself in the backyard? I didn't remember the next door bros playing with it, no wonder it acted pissed off when leashed in the front. What did the owner feel when his dog got murdered? Was that him down there, watching as the dog was rolled onto the bag and then zipped up? The Next Door Bro squatted down and looked at the ground.

"That's hella gross. Check this out, worms and shit."

The city worker ignored him and carried the bag back to the truck. When he or she opened the back of the truck I could see other body bags, maybe a couple dozen--all sizes of animals. The Next Door Bro was still squatting near the ground and poking at it with a stick when the city truck drove off.

I got home maybe an hour and a half after Noah did. Food was made and a plate set down next to an uninterested boy. My son was watching a video of a bad car wreck: A small Nissan had been nearly cut in half by an SUV. Someone was there filming with their phone right after it happened. There were three motionless people inside.

"Hey, I got a video I want to show you."

Noah didn't respond. The person shooting the video was moaning a swear word and lurching off to puke. They handed their phone off to a buddy who filmed the vomit and made an effort to get the lighting right. It looked like the remains of a burger, fries, and a milkshake. My son paused the video and looked over at me.

*Why the fuck are you still here?*

His face said that. Grandma would have lectured that look right off his face. I just squatted next to him and held my phone up so he could see it.

"Why is he in a tank top in January? What a dumbshit."

Watching Noah's face for any emotions: Guilt. Disgust. Intrigue.

Nothing, just a blank. A robot awaiting instruction.

"The guys next door think their dog was stabbed and slashed."

My son shrugged.

"What do they know? They're a bunch of retards."

"Do you know them?" Me, not sure why. The Bros probably *were* retards.

Noah looked over at me with his mother's eyes. Those eyes told me that I was going to lose any argument I started.

"They're just like the kids in my school, just grown up."

He restarted the video. There was so much blood inside the car I had to look away.

"You're assuming that because of the way they look."

Another shrug. I was getting nowhere; I had no game, no Dad game.

"I made the tacos kind of spicy, see if you like them."

Started walking to the door. Almost there my son spoke up.

"Why would you even be on their side, Jeff?"

It was a new tone of voice, surprisingly cold and clinical. The voice of Gerald as he described how much he hated his douchey neighbor.

"I'm not…" *Come on, words; help me do my fucking job.* "Those guys next door probably gave kids like me a lot of shit in school. They deserve to live in that shitty house."

"What about the dog, Noah? Did that dog deserve it? I know you didn't like it when it barked at you."

Probing, pushing a rock over with a stick, scared yet fascinated by what I might find.

"I don't know." The voice of a child, a hurt child, a kid who maybe is trying not to cry.

Why the fuck had I taken him down that road? Did I really think he had anything to do with that dog being murdered? *Maybe he's emotional because he's finally feeling guilty.* Fuck you, Boyman.

I walked back over to his desk. The video of the car wreck had ended; my son selected the option to replay it. From the sidewalk we see the SUV slam into the Nissan so hard it nearly rips in half. Blood sprays the back left window--blood that had been inside another human being a few seconds earlier. It came out of a person who was probably talking about some new pants they got or what they wanted to get for lunch.

The video would go on to get several hundred thousand hits.

And I was there, making it okay to eat tacos and whoop it up as three people died in an economy car. The first night I watched it I was kneeling next to my boy with no idea what to say. Why had I shot the dog being taken away? What was I trying to see in my son by showing him that video? What had made him on the verge of tears?

I had no idea that night, I still don't.

# 16

I was seventeen when Grandma died and managed to live in her house underaged for a few months. Thought I could handle it cause I had a job to buy food--buy food, that was all I could do, I had no idea how to pay the bills or anything like that. By the time the County got to my case I was no longer underage. The house was a mess by then; there was no one there to tell me to do the dishes or vacuum the floors or any of that shit. Grandma's kids that were not my mother came by from time to time. It wasn't to check on me--my aunts and uncles didn't like my mom and by extension didn't really care for me--they were coming by the house to make sure I wasn't throwing parties and to pick through Grandma's shit and take what they wanted. Sometimes they would fight over who got what and all that blahblahblah. I'd just chill in my room on Sleepy McStains and listen to their cheap wars through the walls. Already had a love stain on my futon from fucking some girl who may have been retarded.
Like I said, I did what I wanted even if it was really stupid or thoughtless.
Grandma was dead and it took me years to feel anything but liberated.

I got a second part-time job and had enough money to rent a room in a dirty place with four other Boymen. There were lots of video games, hook-ups with sketchy girls, and microwaved food. I had no fucking idea what to do.

School? Nah, I hella hated that shit for reals. Seventeen became Eighteen became Twenty.

Did some music shit, made some lame moves to get into the viral video game.

A bum got a broken arm and $20 for yelling a racial slur in a BK parking lot. I should have filmed his arm getting broke but I got scared and booked the second those Black dudes started laying into him.

The guy who filmed the arm breaking got 600,000 hits and a big following for a few months. He died in a motorcycle crash--

Someone filmed the accident and the video went viral. Right after that I worked in the office with Gerald. Met Cheyenne when I was in the middle of recovering; she was some chick who showed up with a roommate's girl. For whatever reason we started hanging out and became boyfriend/girlfriend. Ended up in the ER with alcohol poisoning on my 21st birthday. One of the nurses recognized me and laid out a huge lecture--that was the first time Grandma came back to haunt me. I enrolled in Community College, business courses or some bullshit like that. That college thing lasted two months.

I guess I was doing okay at Walmart because they bumped me from 20 to 30 hours a week.

Cheyenne got pregnant: I knew it was mine, knew she wasn't fucking around on me, but I couldn't handle that shit and implied she was cheating or whatever. We had a big fight and that was the end of our relationship.

Twenty-two became twenty-six became thirty-three.

And there I was, shoving some dead dog video in my son's face.

And there I was, confronting my son because I thought that maybe he was a serial killer in training.

I knelt there until he started the car crash video a third time--

Why had Grandma saved me? What good did it do?

It led to *that*, and everything that would follow.

# 17

Saw a woman riding a skateboard and carrying a baby. She may have been twenty or she may have been thirty, with people on the street it's hard to tell.
The skateboarder didn't look worried, her face was blank and hard: That baby may as well have been a bag of Taco Bell. I watched them pass an old Asian man sweeping leaves. Sensing movement, looking at the bush next to me and seeing a caterpillar. Glanced up and the skateboarder with the baby was gone.

I thought about that skateboarder all day at work: Was it her baby? Had she stolen it? How did she see it as okay to ride a board carrying a baby? Those questions as I assembled plastic fans and took plastic off chairs. It's summer now and where I work smells like false cold. My life has become a series of pantomimes--one moment I am setting up workstations and the next I'm heading home.
One second I am looking at the Playing Catch calendar as coffee brews and the next and I am staring at it while grabbing an after work beer.
I can feel the scar across my belly, the heat makes it stretch.
The caterpillar is still reigning over the leaves next to the bus stop.
The way it moves its legs it looks like waving.
One moment I have the taste of my morning coffee in my mouth and the next some candy someone brought into

work. A moment of rage comes from around a corner and moves my arm in arc, sweeping the last school calendar off the fridge. A pissed off hand crushes it, drops it in the trash.

Walking upstairs in the dark, daring witches to come out of the shadows.

And then I'm sitting on Sleepy McStains trying to smell my son through the past. Somedays I feel so lost even Grandma can't find me.

Troubled man, drifting through the days, longing for ghosts.

# 18

February's calendar had silhouettes of Washington and Lincoln. President's Day, didn't need Noah to explain that one. Every time I checked on him it seemed that my son was watching violent videos or playing Boomvest. His grades were all As so I kept my mouth shut; obviously his way of handling his shit was working. I checked on him and brought him food--

The words I needed never came, the ones that would ease his troubles.

I don't fix problems, I exploit them.

Without me Gerald would have ended up some creepy but harmless nerd...

I should have known that he would find my YouTube channel. Not that he ever confronted me, I only found out he had seen them after Gerald became famous.

There were signs, though, lots of them. He started having tantrums about stupid shit, paper jams or no coffee left--things like that. My coworker started keeping to himself more, a dark coil in a nearby cubicle. One day his chair wouldn't adjust and he threw it into the hall.

Someone asked if he was okay--if you watch the video you can see he is too strangled by his own anger even to speak. And then he's looking right at the camera; I see it now, why couldn't I see it then?

The eighth video was called *Gerald Throws a Tantrum*. It got over 40,000 hits.

# 19

There was a big storm after I put the President calendar up. The laughter in the house was joined by a moaning. Noah was so scared he asked me to drag Sleepy McStains into my room. I acted like it was a bad thing but inside...

Inside it felt like a huge step forward: My son was coming to me for protection.

"Who lives in that room between mine and the master bedroom?"

I contemplated making up a roommate he had never met--someone nice, a sunny girl with a welcoming smile. Noah wasn't stupid, that story was.

"I think it's empty."

He was watching me from his bed like a dog that can smell lies.

"That's all I know, Noah. You know where W'Keem and Tyler's rooms are downstairs and they're our only other roommates...aside from the landlords."

"Maybe they use it for storage."

"Maybe."

I don't look at the door to the master bedroom when I walk to our rooms from the stairs. No, I look at the floor or the walls. Years ago I looked at that door once and could have sworn it was glowing--it felt like something was trying to lure me in.

"You look scared."

I pretended to look at my laptop while debating whether or not to lie to my son.

"I've been here years and nothing bad has happened."
The wind shook the house and there was the weird
sensation of being in a dream.
"Got a call from the counselor yesterday."
"Actual yesterday or earlier today; it's not after midnight."
I tried to pull on my Serious Dad face but it didn't seem to
fit.
"Today. She said you yelled something at a couple of
boys."
Noah just stared at me: Flat eyes. Doll eyes.
Feeling in a dream again, waiting for a horrible sharp smile
to form on his face.
"He said you said they would die for being so stupid."
"No," Noah corrected me calmly. "I said they should die
for being so fucking stupid."
And then I saw bruises on the side of his face--why hadn't
I noticed them earlier?
"Did you say that because they beat you up?"
Noah looked down, I could feel him closing up.
"Noah…"
Cue half-ass dad struggling for words to help his son deal
with all the unfairness in the world.
"I know, Jeff, life sucks. Kids are mean. Those retards will
probably find few options when they leave school, join the
military, and get fucked up by the War. It serves them right
and I don't feel bad saying that."
Part of me wanted to tell him that those boys didn't deserve
things ending up like that just because they were school
bullies.

Part of me understood those bullies would probably end up with good jobs and pretty wives.

I hated them for hurting my son but I also resented my son for being different.

Cheyenne and I should have had a bully, not some weird intelligent kid. If I hadn't seen the paternity test I would have guessed that she was fucking some nerd. It would have been like her to get that sort of revenge. Didn't happen that way; I am Noah's Dad--I may have failed him, but I am definitely one of his parents.

And now there are no more storms, just bright summer light. Lots of nights I find myself in his room sitting on Sleepy McStains dreading sleep and another dream of my son waving. With all the bills I can't afford two rooms anymore. They tell me he may not come out of it but I have to think he will.

Cue lost dad sitting on his son's bed crying for the tenth or maybe the hundredth time.

# 20

My hand reaches into my backpack for a snack. I don't
look as I do it because I am pretending that I am
focused/engrossed on jacking in a new workstation--
Expecting cellophane feeling cardboard bent from dozens
of moves from table to bag to pinned on the wall to back in
my knapsack. A birthday card. From Noah. He was still
calling me *Jeff* then--I don't think I even said thank you.
No, I did; details from the past year come and go and then
come back vividly.
There was nothing written on the inside, just what was
pre-printed in the card.
I didn't know he had any money.
I really had no idea he knew or cared when my birthday
was.
Boyman tried to throw the card out maybe a week after
Noah waved.
*Why are you fixated on this stupid fucking card? This is*
*what we get when you let someone in your life.*
Rescued the card and pinned it to the wall. Halfway
through the workweek I pulled it down and put it in my
bag.
Find myself reaching in to touch it, a birthday card with
nothing written inside.

# 21

*A watched pot never boils*, that was another of Grandma's sayings.

It was supposed to point out the uselessness of my childhood impatience but it only made things worse. I couldn't wait until I got out of school and her stupid house. When she died I felt nothing, not even relief. It took a couple of years before I cried over her death. Looking back it was more of a selfish cry because I missed having someone to help me deal with my shit. I never had any cliches that I shared with Noah. I told myself that saying shit like "A watched pot never boils" would just add to his frustration--

Maybe I was lazy, maybe I didn't care enough.

The possibility of the last one will haunt me the rest of my life.

Noah's hair got longer, it got so most of his face was covered by this brown fringe. I wondered if it was to cover up acne but ten is too young for that sort of thing, right? There were times I caught him interacting with other kids. No, interacting wouldn't be the right way of describing it. Cue boy weaving awkwardly through crowds nervously tugging at the straps of his backpack. Maybe he wasn't Gerald; there wasn't any desperate sports talk or awkward jokes.

And what happened in Idaho?

As the months passed I kept building up in my mind what crimes my son had either endured or committed--
There had to be animals involved, maybe he had killed someone's dog.
Serial killers always start off with killing animals, right? You have no idea how much I hate myself for having thought that about my son.
I couldn't help it just as I felt compelled to check his room for the chopping knife. Noah was slipping away from the rest of us: I saw him, playing Boomvest on his phone, sinking deeper into a bottomless lake. In desperation I finally told him my story; walked right in his room and peeled off my Joy Division t-shirt.
We had never seen each other even half-naked so I had his attention.
"See this red line right here?"
The twists his face made could have been fear--was he scared I was getting naked to molest him? Was *that* what had happened in Idaho?
"I'm trying not to look at all the hair…"
A joke, good, he probably just wondered what the fuck I was doing.
"Pay attention, this is important."
Grandma's voice or at least her firm tone, it felt good coming up my throat.
Noah rolled his eyes and turned in his chair to give me the majority of his attention.
"This is a surgery scar. This one, this is where the bullet went in."

My son sat forward to get a better look. There was an
expression I had never seen on his face: Awestruck.
"I'm showing you this because I'm worried about you,
Noah…"
I could tell he wasn't hearing my words, he was just seeing
a spot on my body where a bullet had gone in. It was easy
to see that it was cool as fuck to him but I also got the
feeling that he wasn't getting the message. Maybe I should
have left my shirt on.
"Is there one in the back? An exit wound?"
"No. The bullet is still in there."
"Wow, that's cool."
"No, it's not. I could have died."
Where was I going with that?
*I am telling you this story because I am concerned you will
end up hurting a bunch of people. That you will create
wounds like this in other human beings.*
Yeah, that would really earn my son's confidence.
"Noah, I have no fucking idea what I'm doing; I know you
have picked up on that."
I put my shirt back on and sat on Sleepy McStains.
"I'm worried about how isolated you are--"
He was just sitting there and I saw his face go from
impressed to guarded.
It was easy to see that my son understood where I was
going with the conversation--was he really ten? How was
someone so young so aware?
"Noah--"
"You keep saying my name--why do you keep saying my
name?"

"I don't know, just let me finish, okay? I worry about you watching all those violent videos and playing Boomvest. I think you're detached from what violence is really like--"

"And what, you think because I like being alone and doing this stuff I'm going to hurt people?"

His face was still cold but his tone of voice had changed-- He was a ten year old boy again, a scared and sad kid who realized that his father thought there was a monster inside him.

*And Father of the Decade award goes to...*

Words--why were they so easy for you, Grandma? I have your DNA, why the fuck don't those wise words come naturally to me?

"I'm just worried, that's all. We don't talk, I have no idea how to talk to you; you're so smart, I'm not..."

"Yeah, I noticed."

A joke: That was good, right? If he was pissed off at me he wouldn't have been joking, right?

"The thing is...the guy who shot us was not a bad guy. He was a good person who dealt with a lot of shit and it hurt him enough that he snapped--"

"Did you know him?"

"We worked together...."

We worked together for a few months. I saw his face every day; the shit he was dealing with must have been sketched into his face. Another human being in misery--what do we do these days? We look away. I did that, I helped create the shooter by not talking to him like I should have been talking to another human being.

No, I also had an active hand in creating the shooter.

Thinking about this shit more details are falling out of a room I thought was locked up.

That door was still closed when I was sitting on Sleepy McStains talking to my boy.

"People at work don't really know each other, they just know the people we pretend to be at work."

Recognition on my son's face followed by a nod. The nod felt good; we were definitely talking again.

"Yeah, that's how it is at school, too."

My son was a boy again, I really wanted to hold his hands in mine for some reason--

Should have just done it--maybe that once was my only opportunity; I've done it since then but it isn't the same.

A bomb went off next to a velvet painting store. The blast caused one woman's brains to spatter all over a painting of a tiger.

"Those paintings look weird."

Knelt next to him close enough to smell that he needed to change his clothes.

Couldn't say anything; my son might not let me get so close next time.

"I think they're supposed to be velvet paintings. It was a thing in Mexico a long time ago. Hey, you're almost up to level 30--only eleven more to go."

My son looked over at me and rolled his eyes.

"Eleven? No, more like twenty."

"They found more levels?"

He turned back to his game as he shook his head.

"Yes, Jeff, they found more levels."

# 22

A couple of nights after that velvet painting got covered with brains...

"I wish your great-Grandma was here."

That said under my breath, frustrated that Noah was ignoring me.

"How old was she when she died?"

That was a good question. Grandma always seemed really fucking old but I know she couldn't have been more than sixty-five.

"I was seventeen. My Mom had me really young, like fifteen or something--"

"Name. City where she died."

I gave Noah that information and he started doing magic on his laptop.

"53. It says there she died in an accident."

An accident. I reached under my shirt to scratch at my scar. Noah looked uncomfortable--guilty? Watching all those car accident videos when that might have been how his great-Grandma died?

"That's all it says, *accident*. What happened?"

"It wasn't an accident. They put that in papers to keep s-things private, things families don't want anyone to know."

"Was it a drug overdose?"

I imagined Grandma shooting up and almost laughed.

"She was shot."

"Holy fuck."

I almost got on him for the swear but realized the way Grandma died deserved a *holy fuck*.

"Was she in an office or something? A mall where some kiosk salesman snaps or something?"

"No."

Fifteen years, twenty--whatever the fuck it was it didn't matter. Grandma had been nothing but good to me and I had been a dick to her.

"Are you crying, Jeff."

"Sorry...no, no office or mall but a guy did snap. She was seeing some guy. Turned out he was married and Grandma wasn't down for that. She broke up with him. He waited for her down the street."

And shot her in the driveway. I wasn't home. She had wanted me to be but I was a big man so I did what I wanted--

The bullet hit an artery and she bled out in her own driveway.

Maybe she was crying out; my bedroom was in the converted garage ten feet away.

If I had been there I would have heard it and maybe I could have called 911 and she would have lived.

You have no idea how many times I have told myself that over the years.

The neighbors heard the shots and called the cops right away. It took the cops nearly twenty minutes to get there...for *fucking gunshots*. They took Grandma to the hospital in the cop car because it was clear waiting for the ambulance was a death sentence. It didn't matter. The doctor told me even if she had been shot in the hospital the damage to the artery was too bad to fix.

But I didn't hear that--I never have and I probably never will.

If I had been in my room, been there to care for Grandma like she cared for me, I could have called 911 and an ambulance would have magically appeared and Grandma would have been okay.

The tears just came, there was no stopping them.

I knew Noah didn't want to deal with that shit so I left his room.

# 23

"Hey, bro, I've got a date for my penis enlargement surgery."

How long had Tyler been in the kitchen? How long had I been staring at the Playing Catch calendar? If he noticed that I had rescued it from the trash and kind of smoothed it out before putting it back on the fridge he never said anything.

"Awesome."

He is walking towards the fridge so I move away and pantomime getting a bowl and bag of cereal. Everything is a pantomime these days even when it's really happening.

"Hey...have you ever heard any weird sounds in this house?"

Tyler has the fridge open when he turns towards me. I can't see his dick through his workout pants--is he wearing underwear? His expression is as if I have said something weird or maybe the sounds are something he tries to block out.

"I don't know, man, I just wonder if this house is haunted sometimes."

It feels like a jinx saying that: *This house is haunted.*

My roommate turns back towards the fridge and reaches in to grab one of his oversized energy drinks.

"This house isn't haunted, bro, we are."

# 24

Maybe her number had changed--someone yelling in my ear that I had *the wrong fucking number* would have been a relief. Sitting in a cubicle on a chair still wrapped in plastic as "Baker Street" comes from someone's radio.
No, her number hadn't changed, that would have been too easy.
The song was going into the cheesy sax break when Gail picked up. Her emphysema rasp had gotten even grainer like an old record picking up more scratches.
"You want me to take the kid?"
Like her voice Gail's sneer hadn't changed--it was such a potent thing I could easily hear it over the phone.
"No. There's something that has been bugging me for months--why did they kick Noah out of Idaho?"
The sneer was gone; it was impossible to tell what version of her ugliness was on the other end of the line.
"You didn't ask Cheyenne?"
Fucking hag. Why was I even asking her? Was knowing about Idaho that important?
Baker Street went into the guitar break. It's a fierce solo for such a laid back hippie song, I could relate to the savageness of every string bend.
"She...Cheyenne and I had other business to discuss."
The chuckle; I had forgotten about Gail's mean little chuckle.
The splinter that surprises you when you walk across a wood deck barefoot.

She hates me. I could call her every name there is but Gail has every right to hate me.

"She probably tried to remind you how much you screwed up. Good for her."

The sound of a cigarette being lit: *Work on that cancer you fucking bitch. Die soon.*

I'd be a shitty Buddhist.

"Yeah, she was pissed and she has every right to be. I'm not that 22 year old kid anymore, I'm trying to do the right thing here."

But the damage was done. Everything bad I had done in the past, the weight was *there*. The sound of butterflies being broken--dozens of them, hundreds of them--mic'd up and run through huge speakers.

"It's too late. You've fucked that kid up, you see that, right? Even a selfish prick like you can see that. Yeah?"

Gail wasn't yelling. No, every word was carefully pronounced and slowly slid into the conversation like a knife dripping with poison.

"Maybe."

I saw Noah in my head and replayed all the hurt I had felt coming off him since we met at the bus station.

I replayed that moment with the beer and the shitty diaper. Fucking hag, there was no way I was going to cry during the call.

Baker Street had been replaced by the Pina Colada Song. I fucking hate pina coladas nearly as much as being reminded of shit I already feel bad about.

"He chased a deer away."

"What?"

A long drag away, I could tell the sneer was back.
"He saw they were going to shoot it so he started yelling and waving his arms. The deer ran off."
"They were hunting a deer and Noah scared it off?"
*The deer ran off and there was trouble for me.*
I thought of the dead dog in the neighbor's yard, the missing knife, how I had forced Noah to watch the video--
*Father of the century award goes to....*
"That kid...he's hopeless. Weird. He's a lost boy and that's all your fault. In a few years he'll probably take a gun to school and shoot up the other kids--"
I ended the call but could still hear her voice.
Not yelling, that would have been easy to block out and Gail knew it, she took her time and made every word count.
*In a few years he'll probably take a gun to school and shoot up the other kids.*
Fuck you, you hateful bitch.
I focused on Noah waving his arms to save that deer. He had to have known how much shit he'd get for doing that. My son was a good kid--not that I had anything to do with it.
I wish I could have taken credit, but I couldn't.

# 25

I had a dream of my son waving. I was inside a building
and he was outside--
But it wasn't my son and it wasn't a dream.
It was Gerald, in the parking lot at work moving his arms.
Yelling.
He started to move away from the windows built into the
exit doors. I have spent a long time trying to figure out
what was going on in his head. Maybe Gerald's first
thought was run out into the nature area next to the parking
lot.
He started to, changed his mind, and ran into our office.
Bill Jackson--the man with the guns who changed our
lives--followed.
Bill Jackson, a manager I hated and had been messing with
for months--
After the shooting his wife tearfully recalled their last
conversation being about the gay porn she found in his
car--
Gay porn that was only there because I knew Bill never
locked his car.
It took me a long time to forgive Gerald for leading the
shooter to us when it should have been me...
You know, asking *others* for forgiveness.
The cops said Bill wasn't even planning to shoot anyone.
No, he was only planning to shoot *himself*--a note in his car
said so.
And then Gerald knocked on the window of his car.

Bill had found peace and was ready to end it all--
And that greasy asshole started banging on his window and
yelling.
That gave Jackson the idea to take some people with
him--maybe he made the connection between the gay porn
and his unlocked car and the fact a lot of people at work
hated his guts. Gerald ran through the doors and down the
hall yelling about Bill and guns. Like idiots we all ran out
to see what was going on. Gerald was maybe twenty feet
from me when he was hit. His arms were out like he was
trying to embrace God and his face made a few changes in
the space of a moment:
Fear. Pain. Bliss.
It was as if he understood that he was about to be free from
all the hurt in his life. In that moment I saw him for who he
really was; just a sad nerd, not a bad guy, maybe even
sweet and caring in his own awkward way.
And he was dead before he hit the floor.
One of the bullets that struck him passed through his body
and still had enough force to lodge in mine. They dug
around with the hope of removing it but it's in a dangerous
place. Gerald's blood and tissue were on it when it hit
me--I think about that sometimes.
His blood and tissue will always be inside my body,
circulating.
Gerald saw a man with a gun and ran towards a building.
But it wasn't Gerald and he wasn't running towards where
people were.
It was Noah, waving his arms to distract another boy--a kid
from another school who had showed up with a gun. Some

kid who had been beaten up by Noah's classmates at a mall.
The same ones who had given Noah so much shit.
My son saved some of them. He was really brave and then realized what he was facing and tried to run. The boy with the gun shot him in the back. After he shot my son his gun jammed and the security guard was able to tackle him.
Most of those kids were safe, not my boy.
One bullet can do a lot of damage. I remember the story of when Andy Warhol was shot. This crazy ass chick shot him with a little gun. It was a little bullet but it bounced around and fucked all sorts of inside stuff up.
Same thing happened with Noah.
*We'll just have to wait and see.*
They told me that three weeks ago, nothing has changed.
A boy, too small to be so close to death--asleep. Maybe forever.
You know...I take back what I said about being unsure--
You know, when I said I had my doubts that I even loved him.
I do, it's just terrifying to admit it--to face it.
To love someone so much and know they may never wake up.

I had a dream last night of my son waving. He was standing in short grass between two buildings--
Was he waving at me? Was he smiling? No. My son was in trouble.
When this shit gets really bad I have these crazy thoughts.
No, thoughts is the wrong word, these are *certainties*.

The bullet that killed Gerald also killed me and God is punishing me for tormenting Bill Jackson enough to shoot eleven people. Maybe this is my eternity, seeing the person I love the most gunned down over and over and over.
It hurts, I deserve it.

# Rage Room

How much more grievous are the consequences of anger

than the causes of it?

--Marcus Aurelius

# Sunday 9 P.M.

This is best way I can describe my anger:
Imagine a beast that lives in a remote lake. Sometimes the
creature keeps to the depths, hibernating, but sometimes--
Sometimes it explodes through the surface in a fury.
This lake is on the edge of a remote village. In the past, the
monster was younger and more wild and would destroy the
village on a regular basis. The villagers would just slap
their homes together--what was the point of building a
house with care understanding that the monster would
probably destroy it? Eventually the beast aged and the fire
turned to embers. Maybe it had some self awareness and
consequently felt guilt for all the things it had smashed to
ruin. The beast gained some self control and stuck to the
depths of the lake. The village was wary at first but as the
years passed its inhabitants grew comfortable that the
beast's rages were becoming rarer. The villagers built
better houses and spent more time on the shore of the lake,
fearing less and less that an errant tentacle would sweep
their precious children into legend. The beast is still there,
though. This is something I forget when I imagine the
beautiful village or the surface of the lake without a single
ripple on it: *The beast is still there*. It is still down there
and it is still a monster even if it isn't doing anything--
I was complacent; I shouldn't have been satisfied with the
beast sticking to the depths, I should have tracked it down
and killed it.
If you are reading this the village is nothing but rubble.

# Sunday/Monday Midnight

My bags are in the door and the world is silent now.
Already, I want to go back.
Everytime Sunday becomes Monday it is like this; the
celebration leaves the alcohol as magic potions turn to
poison. This point of the clock always reveals me being
pulled out of a dream. There I was, drinking a good Pinot
or Cabernet, laughing with friends--
But the minutes became hours in a vicious way and the
delicate reds have become savage ambers--cut rate whiskey
from a plastic bottle.
And I am alone.

It has become impossible to ignore the man I am becoming.
Strong emotions are like radiation: A small amount can
remove a questionable growth, a large amount can destroy
a city. This is why I am writing about this week: The plan
is to document the next five days and *not* spend the
following weekend drinking and getting lost in memories.
No, next weekend will be spent analyzing this five day
sample of my life and determining what can be done. I am
also hoping for gold amidst the debris, finding a good man
beneath all this hurt and anger, a man who can sweep up
this mess and move on stronger than before.

A text comes in from PrivatePurge LLC: If I book my
fourth session there will be a twenty percent discount. The
text is deleted without a thought. The glass comes up to my

mouth but the smell of the alcohol has become grotesque to me--

Is there anyway out of this? Is there...or am I just deluding myself?

Maybe I was wrong giving up after my third session, maybe I wasn't opening myself up enough to purge everything out.

Now I am obsessing over that stupid text.

I am obsessing over it and remembering a time when hope came much easier.


*It's another idiotic fad, these people are gullible.*

Those thoughts while watching a news segment on rage rooms. There wasn't any footage of people being violent, just the outside of a drab industrial building and a quick shot of a happy looking woman holding a bat over her head.

*Probably an actress, a shill hired by the people who run the rage room.*

I recall switching off the news feeling superior to what that woman represented; I was an educated person who could deal with their issues using logic and long proven techniques, not fads.

Logic didn't stop me from slamming a door so hard a window broke.

Long proven techniques didn't stop me from kicking the dumpster and scaring my neighbor.

My fine education wasn't enough to keep me from ripping the door off a kitchen cabinet.

There I was, a splinter in my hand, a shattered piece of wood on the linoleum--

There I was, a man who believed he knew the limits of his anger only to feel an invisible line moving over the horizon.

The first session in a rage room was liberating: I beat the shape and purpose out of a flat screen. The aluminum bat that destroyed it was so worn you couldn't tell what brand it was. Maybe it was worn because it had been through hundreds of ball games--

Or, maybe it was worn because it had been through hundreds of flat screens.

The tape was discolored from sweat and I didn't want to touch it at first. Touching it created an unwanted intimacy with a stranger, their bodily secretions and the rage that had led to those secretions.

I spent the first couple of minutes holding the bat by the thick end, looking at the darkened tape.

*I cannot be like the person whose sweat discolored that tape, I am--*

Better than them?

The memory of the shattered cabinet door proved otherwise.

Considering the advantages that I've had in my life I was *worse* than them.

There was the broken door, there was the look of fear on my neighbor's face--

Those two things got me past my hesitation: I gripped the tape and broke that flat screen down to its most basic of components, striking at smaller and smaller pieces of plastic.

A buzzer sounded and my fifteen minutes were up.

Dropping the bat as if I had just struck a home run you could see the tape was even darker than when I had started--

How had fifteen minutes gone so fast?

My back hurt as if I had strained something and there was a feeling creeping in...a darkness, a *weight* where there had been the sensation of liberation and power.

Looking from the bat with the stained tape to the shattered bits of plastic on the floor reminded me of mobile phones--

Mobile phones reminded me of my students--

*Don't think of them when you are in here. It's like staring into a haunted house, something bad will follow you home.*

Catching myself I slammed that door closed.

I forgot to lock it.

Outside the room a woman was waiting with her visor and bat. She had grey hair and a dark blue pantsuit. The lady in the visor looked like someone's grandmother, a grandmother who was about to release years or decades of frustration. I would have watched but there are no windows in the rage rooms: Windows can make you self conscious of all the ugliness you are releasing, ugliness we like to believe is so well hidden that no one knows it exists.

The first time I destroyed a flat screen it started off amazing.

Twenty minutes later there was an ordinary man standing at a bus stop feeling--

Like he had cheated a friend out of a small amount of money.

Like he had masturbated to a nude picture of a girl who may or may not have been underage.

Like--in an attempt at letting out some darkness--he had tossed kerosene on what had been a modest fire.

It was a beautiful day, though. Crows circled calling out and then settled in branches. The afternoon was sunny and warm and the bus was nearly empty. Good things, things I recognized as being worthy of gratitude. Maybe a smile formed on my face. Maybe my feelings shifted from doubt to optimism, weight being released like a submarine clearing its ballast tanks.

# Monday 6:00 A.M.

I was barely awake when Indenture-Temps called. My
handler's voice was like the blinds being thrown open
when one is hungover.

"This is a very early phone call," I said without thinking.
He had been smiling when he introduced himself; I could
hear that the smile had shifted from a light to a blade.
"I'm sorry, is this inconvenient for you?"
I had to remind myself of three things in that moment: That
I needed the man on the other end of the call. That people
can pick up on facial expressions over the phone--
And that there were bubbles arising on the surface of that
remote lake I mentioned earlier.
"No, of course not. How may I help you?"
"Well, we're a little concerned about you and wanted to
make sure you're okay."
And I knew why he was calling--
People had already talked to me about it, I had already
bowed and scraped and been contrite but it was clear that I
had to grovel a bit more.
The smile on my face became tighter, started to ache.
Desperate to keep it tacked on I imagined that I was no
longer talking to my handler but instead a friend from the
old days: William. I imagined William in one of his fine
button down shirts as we drank wine on his veranda.
No, I was not discussing how in a moment of enmity I
smacked a vending machine; we were discussing our plans

for a trip to Santa Fe during the summer recess. Brilliant light in a dozen shades of red.

"You still there, buddy?"

And I was back in my shabby apartment having a conversation with a shabby man.

"Of course."

Why couldn't I have been allowed to enjoy my last half hour of freedom before leaving for the bus stop? I somehow managed to say the right words and bow and scrape to the end of the phone call. After setting my phone aside I stared across the room still smiling. The old ones in the village recognized a smell in the air, the scent of a monster coming close to the surface.

*Don't I have every right to be angry? Look at how I have to shape smiles and lick the rump of this plastic man. Look where I am teaching now; I used to instruct students who wanted to learn or at least pretended they wanted to learn.* Beneath the self-righteousness there is an understanding that I am responsible for where I am. If I can admit that then I suppose it is a sign that I am healing from the betrayal.

If I can admit that it is surely a sign that I am still in control.

# Monday 12:00 P.M.

I get through the morning. Everytime I find myself getting frustrated I don't let my anger build--
This is easier on Mondays, I am not yet broken down.

The first time I destroyed a flat screen it was amazing. It felt good rising from the pond and turning houses and shops into rubble--
And then a buzzer broke the spell and I saw all the pieces brutalized out of unified shape and broken bodies ground into red puddles.
Seeing what I was, slowly reversing back into the depths. Telling myself that all that heady rage was gone and I was back in control.

Days passed in a cycle of food then work then more food and whatever series I was binging on. I brought work home; not just papers to grade but the emotions that had led me to shatter the first flat screen into smaller and smaller components. In the beginning I had been able to talk myself down from fits of anger:
*They are not bad kids. It's their generation, always in their phones--don't be so judgmental. Most of them are still getting their work done properly, why can't you let it go? It's ego thinking that what you are telling them is so important and that the worlds they travel to in those small squares of plastic are insignificant.*

I told myself that but the feelings still came. Came and grew and set roots deeper and deeper. Something big has grown, something I could have just ripped out early on but would take an enormous piece of equipment now. You know how these things go: We see that we have a problem and feel good that we recognized it--*I see that I am a monster therefore I am redeemable.* We feel even better when we make a small step to address it--*I got the Larry Listens app on my phone, I think I am working things out and on the road to recovery.*

It's all a lie, of course, things we tell ourselves to create the illusion that we are still in control.

There is a secret part of the campus where I eat my sandwiches. I came upon it by accident and hoped no one would discover it. Between my class and my secret spot I have to run the gauntlet known as the teacher's lounge. They have big friendly voices and smiles but it is clear that they look down on me because I am a temp--

*Tell me precisely which school you went to in order to get your credentials?*

No, I understand that looking down on *them* just fuels my problems.

It is a challenge, though, when no one there cares to converse with any depth or meaning; they only want to talk about food or whatever show they are binge watching. I smile and act as if I am listening but inside I am imagining that I am speaking with my old friends--

People I mistakenly *thought* were friends during the days of wine and sunlight on our island.

Those days are over for me forever; I understand that I need to accept that. When I am in a forgiving mood--or when I realize that I *need* to be forgiving--I tell myself that they are good people who acted weak and I must be the strong one by being forgiving.

Letters have been sent, actual letters with stamps sent by mail: *I hope all is well with you, wishing you the best.* Sometimes they will even earn a reply--by email. A couple of pithy sentences easily seen through. Contrived smiles that probably hurt them like the one I wore through that phone call.

# Tuesday 6:00 A.M.

The morning routine begins at 5:30. In the old days I would open the blinds and watch the birds stirring in the backyard. There is no backyard here, just a small balcony that overlooks a dying lawn. Beyond it is the parking lot and the battered cars that cruise it playing loud rap or country music. There is no point in opening the blinds here, no point in letting the outside world in any earlier than necessary--*this* world, scraped raw of any finery.

I booked a second session in a rage room. Maybe if I got the monster to over-exert he would have a heart attack and die…
That thought was funny for a moment but the moment has long passed.
The first time I destroyed a flat screen it was amazing but the second time I destroyed one the sense of release had diminished.
The innocence was gone and the illusion shattered, broken into pieces like that forty-eight inch set.
The buzzer sounded and I could feel the discolored tape against my flesh again.
The strain in my back felt more severe, like I would be carrying the damage the rest of my life.
There was a black man who looked like a professor waiting outside with his own bat and visor and I nearly warned him off--

*Don't even go in there. You can't get rid of it, if you're here it has gotten too deep; there is no hope, no cure for this sickness in so many of us.*

He looked up at me and smiled. It was clearly his first time so I smiled and hoped the smile didn't look as forced as it felt.

And then there was a man standing at a bus stop. If you looked at him you'd see a normal looking guy in normal clothes looking down the road for his bus.

Inside, though, he was scrabbling with a pile of mismatched pieces trying to put together something solid and real: Genuine inner peace. Control over emotions growing more and more volatile. Sanity.

Two cars have pulled alongside each other to have a musical argument as I drink my coffee. The world--I have to face it again. It is waiting for me, there is no way around that.

# Tuesday 12:00 P.M.

*I will get through this day and I will get through this week.*
*Tuesday is when it starts getting hard, when I start feeling*
*beat down, start feeling hopeless.*
*I can get through this as I have gotten through it many*
*times. This weekend I will go through this account, take*
*notes, and figure out a way to look at this whole situation*
*and deal with it in a more positive fashion.*

The email I got this morning didn't make matters any
better. Why did I reach out to mother and father again? I
tell myself it is to be the forgiving person, someone who is
past their anger, but the bottom line is that I wish I could be
their son again.
*We do not understand why you are writing to us again. Do*
*you expect us to forget how you let us down and*
*embarrassed us? Please do not trouble us any more.*
Please do not trouble us--
I imagine a cement truck obliterating their car, see the
horror on their faces and then blood spraying all over the
left side windows--
No, that is not fair; I can't think such things--they are small
and weak which is why they are acting this way.
Hearing voices nearby I stop eating my sandwich. Why
does the world have to seep in when I am trying to sort
through this mess and get through the day?
I close my eyes, imagine walking across the campus when I
was in university. Everyday seemed sunlit and the future

seemed boundless. Memories were stockpiled, good memories that added to the beauty in my life.

Now those memories have taken a new form: Barbed wire wrapped around an engine block and one's leg before they are shoved off a dock.

Looking down, I see that I have kneaded my sandwich into a formless mess.

The cigarette smoke and shabby laughter find cracks and rush in like water colored by a million drownings.

# Wednesday 6:00 A.M.

The first time I destroyed a flat screen it was amazing.
The second time was almost satisfying.
The third time was due to Jacob and the circle…
Jacob and his golden motorboat, recklessly doing loops
around the pond, churning the water and sending pings into
the depths where the monster sleeps.
A golden boat for a golden boy with the right smile and a
perfect throw.
*Jacob's a good kid, you need to give him a chance.*
My old handler from Indenture-Temps, issuing an order
that was supposed to sound like a suggestion. And I bowed
and scraped because there is no tenure for me, no security;
I am just a temp on assignment.
Despite the university I worked at.
Despite all my performance reviews that glittered as if
coated with precious metal.
Are they still in files there or were they discarded like me?
*Jacob's a good kid, you need to give him a chance.*
Perhaps Jacob seems like a good kid to those who care for
him, those who can look past how he is always wrapped up
in his phone or exchanges with his classmates.  I see them
looking at each other, looking up at me, and then looking
back at one another with a smirk. No words need to be
spoken, it is written clearly on their faces: *Not even a real
teacher, a temp. Cheap clothes, no cologne, flaccid shape
from cheap food. Poor skin.*

At best I am an inconvenience to them, at worst a pathetic
joke--I get that--
But *they're* the ones attending a shabby public school.
I have been on *the inside*, on an island of exclusivity.
I have been close to those who will actually shape the
world; Jacob and his smirk buddies will always be on the
outside.
At best they will end up in stressful middle management
jobs, at worst in the service industry.
The sad truth is that these are their golden years. Maybe
they should be allowed to have them, perhaps I need to
look past my feelings and see that.
In calm moments such as these I understand that my anger
is not about them-- But then I hear the roar of a vicious
motor and smell the exhaust of a boat at full throttle doing
loops above me. I close my eyes, try to make the boat
smaller and smaller, hundreds then thousands of feet above
me. Most times my efforts fail. Sensations come on and it
feels like hundreds or even thousands of bees are stinging
me; there is no choice but to stop the intrusion by rising
from the darkness and destroying what has ended my
peace.

# Wednesday 9:00 P.M.

Wednesday is always the worst day of the week.
I went through my lessons. The students either looked
bored or cast one another knowing looks or did things on
their phones. Disciplining them was not an option for two
reasons:
I understood that Indenture-Temps would reprimand me for
"being hard on the students" again.
Secondly I knew that I could not be fair and calm with
them, that if I addressed their indiscretions it would be with
fury--
I daydreamed of bellowing at them, addressing their
failings with such force that they fell from their chairs.
Feeling my anger stretching its legs for a long run I shifted
daydreams. I followed the light streaming through the
windows back to the university. Instead of forty students I
was addressing a dozen. None were staring at their friends
or their phones, they were engaged and asking
questions--we were having a real dialogue--
That's what I miss the most about my old position: Seeing
those young people who will shape the world radiating
curiosity and intelligence.
Did I close my eyes? I heard laughter, someone cued a
recording of flatulence on their phone. The darkness inside
me shuddered to life and I felt sparks in my blood.
And then we were all saved by the bell.

The third time a flat screen lost its form I was no longer in the moment: It seemed idiotic, nothing more than a pantomime. I became aware of the texture of the aluminum bat and the sweat under my arms and how the room smelled like air freshener. For the first time I noticed a banner pinned to one of the walls: *We're here.* The font was calligraphy and I got the odd sensation of dissimilar worlds intersecting.

My time wasn't up so I didn't walk out; my instincts were telling me that the door was locked until the buzzer went off--
I didn't want to face the fact that I was trapped in there with my rage.
That possibility never came to mind when I gave my debit card information to pay for the session. *Debit* card, all my credit cards were exhausted during my search for work. Another instance of all the finery being scraped from the world.

When I went into the first rage room I felt like an overheated hiker coming upon a remote lake. There was delicious relief as the cold water hit my skin and I swam out towards the middle. No one was around, it was just me and my pleasure--
And then I became aware of the possibility of things living hundreds of feet below my tiring limbs, hungry things.
I wasn't alone, something had been stalking me from the first moment I threw myself in the water--

And now it was rising towards me; who knew how large it was.

I was no longer a man with free will and purpose and strength, I was just an inviting meat shape weak and far from land.

How had I been so foolish? How had I been tempted by something a logical man would have understood was a trap?

The buzzer sounded and I awoke. I am still awake.

# Thursday 6:00 A.M.

Tomorrow night will be a full moon. Last night I drank whiskey and watched videos as the monster in the lake moved through the shadows in the back of my mind. The whiskey was in a plastic vessel. The emptier the bottle got the more the plastic would give; I found myself compulsively squeezing it as I got drunker and drunker. There was the understanding, now proven, that this morning would be ugly.

Tomorrow is a Friday--if I can get through today and tomorrow then I will have the weekend to get my business in order--

*Get your business in order*, Malcolm said that to me on my last day on the island--the last day I lived in a house made of bricks following the last night of drinking wine with friends as the smell of jasmine filled the air.

*Get your business in order*--like he was in a position to judge, as if he were some flawless being whose excretions had no stink.

Allowing the beast to rise to the surface in this manner does no good, I understand that--

A buzz, however, is cutting through that understanding: Millions or even billions of killer bees drifting over the horizon. Last night there was a battle, Clan McGregor rising with a war cry to stop the swarm. I was feeling good, daydreaming about the library back at the university, only to see the brave McGregors decimated by a cloud of fury.

I swear I am feeling dozens of bee stings all over my body as I write this.
The stings become paper cuts and then a ghoul creeps up from behind to shove me in a pool full of rubbing alcohol.

Despite his hypocracy I understand that Malcolm was correct; I *must* get my business in order.  I need to develop fortitude and work through everything I am feeling at this time--
It hurts, though, hurts like nothing I have ever experienced.

Last night I allowed myself an escape by rowing out to the island. I have trained my mind so I can leave this apartment, traveling hundreds of miles and months into the past. I leave this wretched place every Friday evening, there are sun dabbled escapes, fine wine, and light on skin. Beauty is wrapped around me like velvet but by Sunday the fabric grows thin.
An ugly understanding cuts through my bliss; the next time I close my eyes and open them it will be Monday again.
Monday is tolerable but each progressive day breaks me down.
By Friday I am all gritted teeth and coils of sharp metal.
My students think they're anxious for the final bell, counting down the minutes until the week is over. I am counting down the *seconds*.
Behind my desk, clenching my fists, determined to get through to Friday afternoon and--*next weekend*--getting my business in order.

I make that promise to myself every week: *You will survive this week and spend the weekend figuring out how to deal with this, really deal with it. You can get through to Friday afternoon, there is no choice.*

# Thursday 9:00 P.M.

*Where you at, bro? You dead? Seriously, where u at?*
Chase. He wants to believe that he is looking out for a
friend but the truth is he needs to feel like a good guy,
someone who looks out for people. Chase blames himself
for the death of his fiancee. Considering that she was killed
in a workplace shooting that's absurd: He had no idea she
would die when she left that morning, he certainly wasn't
the shooter--grief is strange.

Chase was waiting outside the rage room after my third
session. I must have been making an odd face because he
made an odd face of his own. I asked how many times he
had been in the room and his reply was *twice*. I noticed his
cologne was well-chosen and told him that I'd be out there
waiting for him. It was easy to see that my promise threw
him; Chase backed into the room and closed the door.

Fifteen minutes later he was walking out with the same
face I had probably been wearing a quarter hour earlier. We
looked at each other for a few moments and then one of us
suggested a drink.

By the time the media had caught onto rage rooms all of us
had smashed our second flat screen. We found buddies to
go hunting with or drink with and had a brief period of
companionship. The thing about anger, though, is it is very
personal--each person's anger is as unique as a fingerprint.

Even if we're angry about the same issue we are different people who have been formed by different experiences. Consequently, the connection formed after smashing our third respective flat screen quickly grows threadbare and disintegrates. My companion seemed shallow and was clearly homosexual. His being queer was not the issue, it was that he was not strong enough to accept what he really was. Conversely, Chase didn't understand why anyone would want to be a teacher; so much work for not much money. There were flashes on his face when he looked at me with what was clearly disgust, most likely at my girth and cheap clothes. I considered his job in middle management pointless and vacuous--I didn't say that directly but I'm sure there was a sarcastic remark or two made at some point.

Our friendship was built for two nights out tops. It lasted one night aside from the texts. The first drink was knocked back to kill the awkwardness between us. The second drink was ordered with a degree of uncertainty: *Is there any point in hanging out with this fellow to the bottom of a second glass?* The liquor drowned our differences; we were out to sea together, the two of us on a ship of illusions. I could still see land, however, I do not believe Chase could. Once handed the excuse of intoxication he spoke of his grief and tears nearly came. With my own eyes I let him know that was unacceptable. My companion shook off his feelings and changed the subject. He expressed his weariness at the rage rooms and that he had heard about other outlets such as the Meetings. I probably don't know anymore about the

Meetings than you do: People gather out in the middle of nowhere and let their rage out in a number of ways. I've heard of the Meetings being responsible for fires, explosions, and even homeless meth addicts hunted down like deer.

*I've got a buddy who has offered to vouch for me, he'd probably help you out, too.*

It was clear that Chase was still hoping, still *believing* that there was something out there that would cleanse him off all the darkness inside.

Despite my agreeable smiles and words I had lost that belief.

It was clear when Chase dropped me off he believed we could be pals.

I understood, even through the intoxication, that our differences would return when the effect of the liquor dissipated--

I was alone, truly alone, and trying to stop *all this* with a friendship was pointless.

Chase's enthusiasm for the Meetings did not mesh with my growing belief that stirring the beast in the lake was a bad idea. Maybe instead of letting my anger out I should break it down, try to understand why I am so angry at life and the world and kill the beast once and for all.

That was my thinking as I fumbled for my keys after Chase dropped me off.

That is why I continue to write in this journal or whatever it is.

# Thursday/Friday Midnight

Just watched a video of a man throwing a chainsaw in the air and then attempting to jump out of the way. As I watched it on *Folkz Die* you can probably guess the outcome. My hope is that if I watch these videos of people getting slit open by chainsaws or shot at Taco Bells or dying in car wrecks it will remind me how awful violent death is; how I really need to put the thoughts I have been having out of my head--
It hasn't worked.
I am determined, though; determined to get through tomorrow and spend this weekend coming up with a plan to take care of this once and for all.

There is a beast in my head there is a beast in my desk drawer at work. I never wanted it there. Whatever happens please keep that in mind. They forced that monster on me and it is becoming an extension of my own monster: *This new program will keep the kids safe if violence occurs at our school. Don't you want that? Don't you want more money each month for being part of the program?*
It was part not wanting to say *no* and part that I was treading on thin ice for smacking that vending machine--
Smacking it and yelling a bunch of words you're not supposed to use in a professional environment.
There was also the instance of slamming my classroom door after the principal had a *chat* with me about how I had yelled at a student.

All that in mind, I was surprised when they asked me to be part of the new program.

You would think that I would be the last teacher they would select to keep a gun in their desk drawer.

*It is not their fault. They are not bad people. They are just full of raging hormones and short attention spans.*
I am thinking of the kids in my homeroom, especially the ones that frustrate me the most. When the rage comes I try to imagine them having a great day or smiling happily or things along those lines.

Please believe that I try and imagine them in good situations, I really do.

Those positive thoughts, however, are always interspersed with them lying in pools of blood, their faces wracked with pain and surprise. Why do I get so angry with them? Is it because they are being disrespectful with regard to my instruction? Is it because it irritates me that they don't care one iota about things I consider important?

Is it because they are young and have all these possibilities ahead of them?

I couldn't tell you, that is one thing I will need to sort out this weekend.

Those fatalistic thoughts come and I hear the monster stirring in my heart which wakes the beast in the drawer. I can no longer think about the kids so I focus on whatever lesson we are on, focus on it with a desperation I hope you never experience.

I got through Thursday. A smile somehow formed on my face when I crossed paths with other teachers and even that charlatan the principal. Words came out of my mouth--did I laugh too brightly? There were scores of crows in the trees surrounding the parking lot. A couple of them were calling out as I reached the bus stop.

*One more day to go. I can get through one more day then it's the weekend.*

The crows helped, the trees helped. Nature gave me peace for a few moments only to have a siren shatter it and send sharp angles through the air and into my skin.

It is nearly Friday. In five hours my alarm will be going off and this whiskey which is so nice at the moment will be a curse in my blood. There are bubbles on the surface of the water and growing waves as if a storm is coming in. I should be able to calm the water, right? It is my mind, my own emotions--I can control them, right?

Silence. Always silence.

It took a long time for me to go to the rage room. For so many years I had been telling myself that the beast was something to exterminate or at least keep deep below the surface. I finally understood that I needed help or had to purge it from my system. Taking the bus to that building was facing everything bad inside me. I stood in the parking lot for a long time. There was something up on the wall, a place where letters had been maybe; the building had probably been a department store at some time--

And then I willed myself through a door and into the lobby.
All sorts of people were there: Old. Young. White. Brown.
A girl in a wheelchair, that one made me curious. After the
first flat screen I felt better than I had in months, it felt like
I was exorcising all the darkness that bubbles inside of me.
In the middle of breaking up the second flatscreen I began
to understand that I was kidding myself.
Maybe I should have gone with Chase to one of the
Meetings. Maybe that would have been enough to wear the
monster out and kill him.
On the other hand, maybe the need to vent this rage would
have simply grown and grown requiring larger and larger
acts of destruction.
That thought scared me to the cells; it is nearly too large to
control as it is.
I have to deal with this on my own, there *has* to be a way--
Am I mistaken in believing that people have cured
themselves of rages stronger than mine?
Silence. Always silence.

When I get frustrated with my students I try to imagine
good things for them; it has been getting harder and harder.
Sometimes I open the desk and look down on the drawer
monster as it sleeps.
I close the drawer and hate myself a little bit more.
No, I hate the man I am in moments such as these.

I am drinking whiskey in my last wine glass. Don't recall
what happened to the others, maybe I got clumsy or maybe
I got angry--

There used to be six of them. Saturday mornings I'd see them sitting on the kitchen counter, some with lipstick smears on the rim. That's a good memory: The morning after laughter and fellowship--

Those days are gone forever, I try and face that and it just hurts.

There is no better word than *hurts* in some situations--

Going on and on about this is pointless, I understand that. Perhaps I should leave this room and head somewhere wild like the desert, leave it to nature to either heal me or send one of its many agents to seal me in the earth.

One last little voice is telling me to take three days to get my business together--call in sick tomorrow and then see what therapists are available in my network. Everything I have done in an attempt to control my rage hasn't worked, it's time to go against all my prejudices against psychotherapy and get help.

Tomorrow I will do that, I will call in sick and spend the day finding someone to help get me through all this…

Hearing my voice, as far away as I may be, they will find me--

I have to believe that.

Hearing my voice, they will pick up the monster in the lower notes, track it down in its lair, and aid me in killing it once and for all.

Hand in hand, we will hold our fists aloft in victory with the smell of its blood in the air.

That moment is out there and I have to believe that I can reach it with measured steps: Call in sick. Find someone who can help me. Listen to them, really listen to them, and follow their instructions to feel alright again…

If you are reading this, I didn't call in sick.

# Today's Lesson

# 1

The blackberry thorn going into my skin reminded me of needles; I was on my knees behind the cabin when the present and past began to occupy the same space. Pulling off my glove, I scolded the red dot on my finger and then found myself mesmerized by it: It wasn't just a dot, it was a trigger, a piece of magic taking me back to the time when needles were a regular thing for me.

More memories: A doctor's office. The feel of disposable paper when you lie on it. The smell of rubbing alcohol--Those memories reminded me of a phrase I was obsessed with then:

*Maybe you can only start to live when you stop thinking.*
That was my mantra then, in the needle days--funny how the things that were so important are allowed to just slip away.

I had been waiting for that sentence for months. After ages of useless advice Linda finally gave me those eleven words. I *had* been thinking too much--thinking, worrying. The hope for such a gift was why I had put Linda Listens on my phone. I remember borrowing a friend's debit card to buy the app; if my folks knew I had bought it there would have been conversations and questions and other shit I didn't want to deal with.

*Why would you buy an app instead of talking to us? We'll always listen.*

Yes, they always listened but they never heard me; even in my last year of high school they still treated me like a little kid.

I went inside and washed my finger. The past and the present occupying the same space fucked with the passage of time or maybe just my awareness of it. What had been a lazy sun had grown fleet and was over the hills. I peeled the band-aid on my finger back to remind myself of what it concealed, a wound that with time would become another scar.

The full moon revealed itself slowly. It had been a warm day but a chill came on to keep the dark company. The moon. The needles. Whiskey changed the weight of a glass and I sat at my kitchen doing absolutely nothing. No, I was sipping my drink and allowing the past to overwhelm the present.

Another memory from the needle days: Someone had broken into McDonalds and fucked with all the robots. The burger flippers, the ones where you put your order in--fucked them all up. My folks thought it was some kind of protest. That conversation was interrupted by the doorbell telling us our dinner was on the front porch. The man who delivered our food had a limp and roared off in some beat ass car. Why was he limping? Was it a childhood deformity or a sports injury?
Maybe he got shot--

Maybe he had a good job and one day someone came in and started shooting. It fucked with him; fucked his leg up and his head, too.

I watched his car moving down the street until it was too small to see. My mother called to me from the kitchen no one cooked in. Even now I can smell the dust in the drapes as I backed out of them and the feel of our wall to wall carpet on my bare feet. All the memories I made in those months are still vivid.

McDonalds was in our conversations and on my mind. Their ad for the McSpicy had been blowing up my computer for over a week. At first it looked amazing and I craved it--until I saw the Drip. The Drip changed everything. It was probably supposed to be some sort of hot sauce, a detail to make the sandwich look more real. It did, but not the real they were intending.

*Maybe you can only start to live when you stop thinking.* How long would I obsess about the Drip? What was going to happen in three weeks when I graduated? There was the feeling that the world was hungry for me--why else would they be allowing me to graduate? I hadn't learned anything since starting home school. They gave me tests on things I was supposed to learn and then gave me chance after chance and hint after hint until I passed. The feeling of *not being ready* for post-graduation was intense; I have lost many sensations from back then--desires, beliefs, and hopes--but not that one.

Before I noticed the Drip I had been totally craving the McSpicy. Now it sounds disgusting but I am not in the *now*. I recall grabbing my jacket to walk down to the nearest McDs maybe six or three or nine times.

And then I'd imagine my parents going over the receipt; they checked *every* receipt when I bought stuff on my card. *Spicy? What is this McSpicy you bought? You don't have a gallbladder anymore--do you want to get sick?!*

And those six or three or nine times I'd drop my jacket on the bed and feel defeated, like life was always going to suck and there was no changing that.

# 2

My mouth is coated with whiskey and it is a full moon. I can look at the moon now because I can see that it is just the moon. There was a time I couldn't, when it would appear to be other things. Now I look at the moon and feel a victory, feel strong--"healed" even.

*Maybe you can only start to live when you stop thinking.* Linda gave me those eleven words, a beautiful directive that I hoped would eventually lead me to peace. I had no idea how, but my intuition was that those eleven words would heal me. Maybe I had to believe that. Maybe I just jumped on those words out of desperation. I was tired of having an anxiety attack every time I saw the moon through my window. It was gruelling being outside at night with it filling the sky and daring me to look up. And I would, knowing doing so was the only way to see if I was getting better.

The answer was always *no* back then.

Another memory: Text after text from Linda reminding me about sessions; those eleven words were cheap but they had set loose a pest in my phone that never tired. I wanted to block messages from the app but didn't know how. My folks checked my history so if I looked it up they'd find out about the app and it would be Serious Discussion Time. SDT was the last thing I needed.

The same day the McDonald's robots were vandalized Mom walked in on me when I was rubbing my scar. I didn't even know I was doing it; it's just something I do without thinking even now. I can see her face--she was trying to look loving and concerned but it was easy to see how uncomfortable she was. Mom looked at my face and then down at where I was scratching. The pain and awkwardness she clearly felt became too much to hide; my mother walked out without saying a word.
I felt bad for her, felt guilty as if the whole situation had been my fault.

After she walked out of my room there was a pop quiz on the computer. Most of my answers were wrong but the computer kept giving me hints until I got those answers right. Pass tests, graduate in three weeks--then what? College? My folks weren't sure about that; there had been shootings at colleges, too. Graduate and get a job? Maybe get one of the sign flipping jobs or something in a store that sold weed. There were always jobs in those places that make bombs and other shit they use in the War. Someone had told me there was decent money in that and I got hopeful and then disappointed after learning you need college for those jobs. Now I understand how stupid that short lived dream was: Me--*in a factory*; I wouldn't have lasted a day in a place where loud, sudden noises are part of the job.

Everytime the McSpicy ad came on I had to mute it and look away. The Drip made my skin itch and my limbs restless--it was no longer hot sauce and it was no longer dripping out of a sandwich--

Was that really part of the *then*? In this moment, in this room, it is feeling like the *now*.

# 3

I blame the crows for the blood. They were making a bitter noise when I was pulling out the blackberry vine; the birds distracted me enough to grab thorns instead of a more gentle part of the plant. Another memory of the crows in the tallest tree behind my childhood home. They made a lot of noise and one time my Dad joked about getting an air rifle or something--
He made that joke and then looked guilty and sick to his stomach.
And then both of my parents looked at me and I felt my scar itch--
My Dad never shot at those crows; I couldn't imagine him ever picking up a gun. Before they took me out of school he had talked about getting a handgun to keep our house safe but it was just talk.

I hated my weakness and watched the McSpicy commercial over and over, forcing myself to look at the Drip. It was just hot sauce coming out of the side of a sandwich, I knew that.
And when darkness came it was just the moon in the sky looking down and nothing more. I knew that, as well.
If I knew that then why did it still feel as if insects were cutting paths in my skin and why were my legs spasming?
My therapist said that the feelings would never be over. He slipped when he admitted that and quickly tried to cover his tracks even though it was too late--

*What I meant was that you will keep thinking about this the rest of your life but less and less often. It will be okay, we'll get you through this.*

But he didn't. I got sick of wasting an hour a week in his office that smelled like herb tea and carpet cleaner and came up with some lies of my own. I had all these reassuring smiles and talk about how I was feeling better. It was all bullshit--

They bullshitted me and I bullshitted them back.


Two more fingers of amber in the glass. I pull off the band-aid again, the mark is faint and the blood is gone but I still see it. Are you still there?

*My folks are so oblivious. They just told me about the lady who got Jacob's heart and how she has set up this shelter for feral cats. I wanted to fucking punch them.*

I remember most of the texts I got from R. Maybe it was because my mind was like velcro and everything stuck to it or maybe it's because all her writing was very vivid and ugly beautiful like the lyrics of a band you embrace because they can say the things you have no idea how to express. Whatever the reason I recall every text R sent. We were both friends with Jacob. Maybe he wasn't such a good friend on the last day but he was scared--we were all fucking scared…

And then his heart was in some crazy cat lady.

I Googled her and it turned out that she was totally Miss Right Wing gun lover; guess that worked out pretty good for her. She probably voted for arming the teachers at our old school. I can see her wheeling one of those portable oxygen tanks down to the church where they set up voting booths. In my imagination she is wearing a loud sweater covered in cat hair. And she got Jacob's heart. I wonder if when you get a body part from another person you get any of their memories? I mean, I know memories are made in the brain but it just seems like you'd get *something* from that person. Jacob had a milk allergy; maybe transplant lady barfed the first time she tried to eat cheese after she got his heart. It's a mean thought but at that time mean came easier than I care to admit.

# 4

I woke up to the sound of crows. Someone has cut down a tree around here; a nest was found in ruins which explains why the crows are so pissed off. The band aid came off in the night but the wound is nearly invisible, a dot smaller than a grain. I still see it, though.
The moon has vanished with the break of day but I still see it as well.

Someone gets clumsy and something heavy falls and makes a terrific sound. The past overlays the present with enough substance to block it out--
There is a memory of Mom knocking over something heavy in the garage. I didn't know the cause of the noise at the time, all I knew was the sound, a huge explosive sound, and then I was lying face down on my floor. I could smell the dust in the carpet and see that I needed to clean under my bed--
And then I remembered where I was and the relief was so intense I started crying. Getting up, the movement of my skin made my scar itch. I touched it; it was still a scar--a wound repaired and then healed over. The wound was still there, though, it was only hiding, a ghost in a haunted house waiting for you to let it into your heart.

# 5

Did I tell my folks about throwing myself on the floor? No,
telling them about that situation would have hurt them,
would have been a reminder of something none of us
wanted to talk about or even acknowledge. I wasn't always
so considerate of them. There was the time I learned that
they had taken me out of school; I was so angry I told my
folks that I hated them. Both their faces sagged with
hurt--they had nearly lost me, it was too soon to almost
lose me again. Things haven't been the same since I told
them I hated them. Apologies were offered and accepted
but what was said has changed things, I know that and feel
guilty.

I was still recovering when they took me out of school. The
anger I felt was too intense to ask them why--
*How dare you make that sort of decision when I was too*
*weak to stand up for what I wanted!*
Not that my being strong or weak would have made a
difference. My parents had been swept up in a
*movement*--there had been so many incidents like the one
we went through that a lot of parents had taken their kids
out of school. I was angry at the time but eventually that
anger was replaced with worry for the future: The world
seemed full of noise like shit falling in garages. The world
was waiting to eat me--I know how crazy that sounds but I
felt it. It was safe at home, just hanging out in my room. I

had everything I needed including food delivered to our front door.

All that had been soured by the realization that it couldn't last forever.

Maybe my parents would give me a few weeks or a few months but eventually they would expect me to get a job or go to school or something like that.

The memory of R's text about Jacob's heart going to the cat lady brings up a memory of meeting my friend at the mall. The mall always smelled like popcorn and new shoes. My folks would drive me at first--they'd even leave work to take me--but by the point of this memory they were okay with me taking the bus. I wish they hadn't been; looking back it was probably blowback from saying that I hated them. Maybe I could have stayed in my room and gotten rides forever if I hadn't said that. I can still see their faces; I was high as fuck on pain medication but I remember their faces clearly. Why did I get so angry? Guilt is a restless rider that can carry on for years.

R should have died. She knew that and it messed with her head. That day in the mall my friend showed me her nails. "Look how long my nails are."

It seemed like a good thing; there had been a time when R chewed her nails all the time, chewed them as far down as you can chew them.

"Yeah, good to see you're letting them grow."

"I read somewhere that after you die your nails continue to grow."

No, I had read somewhere that it's *not* your nails growing, it's an illusion created by your skin shrinking back or something like that.

Her having the facts wrong wasn't what was important, it was the *subtext* of what she was saying: R should have died and she obsessed over that. Even when she didn't talk about it you could see a busy brain machine through her eyes. My friend was pretty when you first looked at her but if you looked closer you could see all the hurt and crazy. That day we just sat on a bench for awhile. A group of happy girls around our age walked by all smiles and talked about whatever happy people talk about. I was bitter about their happiness then, now I just wish I could have stolen or even borrowed it for awhile. What R and I felt no one should understand. She should have been allowed to continue being a pretty, happy girl who walked around the mall with her friends talking about shoes and boys and whatever but it didn't work out that way. The pretty she had would quickly flake off and be sucked into the vents of that stupid mall. I wanted to talk to R about what happened when I heard the noise in the garage but knew that would bring her own shit up. We just sat there looking around, too scared to look at each other because we knew we'd see the same shit we were feeling in the other person's eyes.

After we said goodbye I just wandered around. Details were captured by the lazy camera in my head that somehow still remain: *We're Here* written in orange sharpie on the long, spooky corridor to the bathrooms. An old man with green mall walking shoes humming to himself. A cash dollar drifting in front of a Korean restaurant that no one seemed to see. Was it because it was worthless or because most of the mall people had their faces in their phone?

I carried that question and many others on the bus ride home.

# 6

There are always more blackberries to pull. Someone
thought it was a good idea to use them to create a natural
barrier on the west line. Clearly that someone didn't realize
how far those vines can spread. I removed the brambles
with the caution of the recently spurned. Despite that, my
gloved fingers still brushed the thorns which brought back
more needle memories. Not just mind pictures but scents;
the smell of acetone where it didn't belong.
No, not acetone, industrial cleaner. The kind they use in
hospitals.
My body has lost touch with whatever physical pain I felt
in the year of the needles but the smells are still there.

I had an elaborate meal in mind but was weary from
working outside and settled for something simple.
Sometimes--maybe often--I miss the day when all my
meals were delivered. The delivery man with the limp was
the only person who ever rang the doorbell. Hearing the
door I would stop what I was doing and go to the window.
There, my hands would bunch up the drapes enough to give
me a view of the outside world.
*In less than three weeks it will be out there waiting.*
I had no sense of the present in those days; minutes and
hours were consumed by the fear beast inside me rising
from the depths.

Maybe I could deliver food. Sometimes you had to ring the bell and faces would look in yours but most times you just left a bag by the front door--
I could have been another delivery driver with a story that could never be told to strangers. Maybe, at some point on my route, someone with their own story would be watching me from their window; hands bunching up coarse fabric, smelling dust, dealing with fear.

S had the McSpicy commercial on a drive so I got a copy from him. He had no questions; some people are kind enough to give you space when you have a story you don't care to share face to face. The commercial was how I remembered it but the feelings are gone. I forced them out years ago but I remember how much effort it took. There came a point when I made muscles and didn't mute that commercial or look away; I even dared it to make me feel the things I had felt before. Watching the commercial reminded me of that struggle and how R had texted me while I was eating the food the man with the limp had brought us. Crows had been dropping things on her house. Her folks heard sounds on the roof and went outside to check it out. There were lots of crows in the trees, R said thousands but she liked to exaggerate. She watched them for a couple of hours and told me that there were patterns in the way they flew. I realized I loved her and forgot about my food. Not a romantic love, more the frustrating love of caring deeply for someone you know you can't save.

Another memory, one from before R texting about the patterns in crow flight:
*Big Boom Time* wanted to talk to me about what happened at school. Being a minor I needed my folks permission and they wouldn't give it. I acted irritated but it was a relief; I was still a mess and strange voices freaked me out.
They tried to interview R but she couldn't stop crying.

On the same thumb S had leant me there was an online article about all the parents that had pulled their kids out of school in the needle days. That had led to more and more kids taking classes online. At least I could get through my lessons, R lost focus after a minute or two. My guess was that it was because of the coma: They put her in a medically induced coma and that never made sense to me--aren't comas dangerous? Why would you put someone in a coma on purpose? Jacob's Dad had a stroke and went into a coma but he did that on his own, didn't come out of it either. Imagine how fucked up that was for his wife? You lose your son and your husband in the space of a couple days.

At the eleven second mark in the McSpicy commercial they do a close up of the bun and sauce oozes out for between one and two seconds--the Drip. I used to pause it in the middle of those one to two seconds and dare it to become something else; someone's life pooling out onto dirty tile. R gasping in pain and confusion as she lay on her side. The sound of screams in counterpoint to the sound of chairs being shoved aside or falling back with bodies in them. I closed my eyes and opened myself to whatever memories would come. A moon face bright as the sun smiling with what I will always swear was love followed by the side of the moon exploding as if a nuclear bomb had been detonated there. The red mushroom cloud had been followed by the moon quickly setting behind a desk. The memories come like dogs running towards you that never forget your face no matter how long you've been gone. They threw themselves on me and for awhile there was only their weight and hot breath. When I got tired of it the memories were easily pushed away--it's a good thing I made myself strong.

# 7

They never found out who destroyed all those robots at McDonald's.

# 8

I remember three weeks becoming two. The truth was that my folks would have probably let me live there forever; I could have been their invalid child peeking from behind the drapes whenever the bell rang.

No, it was more complicated than that, partially from me saying that I hated them--

Part of it was that we had talked about my issues too many times, Serious Discussion Time at the dining room table we never ate at. My folks would try to look concerned, like they were listening, but to me they just looked uncomfortable. I was different to them, their child and yet not something clean and innocent anymore. I made it home but for a few hours/days/months they were scared they were going to lose me. I was not nearly as bad off as R but my parents hadn't heard the doctor when she said my injury wasn't life threatening--

Their child was shot; there was blood all over me--not all of it mine--and I was in pain and at the hospital. If my parents could have come out and admitted that they were scared to love me I wouldn't have blamed them; it would have been nice if they had been able to admit it, you know? Instead we just read lines like characters in a stupid movie where none of us know the ending.

I clean the dishes from my simple meal and sit at the kitchen table with a glass of whiskey. S probably told everyone about my interest in a seven year old McDonald's

commercial; with few distractions gossip has too high a value around here. I sit in my kitchen but I see another kitchen and imagine a bag of food on the counter--
Maybe our delivery driver had been in the War, maybe every time he passed a playground the sight of sand made his mouth dry and his hands move as if cradling a rifle. I found myself sitting in his passenger seat sometimes when I closed my eyes and dared the edged thoughts to come in.

I remember a time like that: Finding my bag of food in the kitchen and my mother catching me in the hall as I carried it to my room. Now I see her and feel love but as the memory was being made the way she moved and smiled it seemed like I was a wild thing that she had spied in the yard and regretted trapping.
"Let me know if they got your order wrong, your father didn't get bacon on his--not that I agree with his eating bacon."
I can see her rolling her eyes and smirking in the way she did when things were different, before I told my parents I hated them--
I couldn't decide if I wanted to hug her and never let go or run out of the house in one last attempt to save myself. This is how it was every time we ran into each other.
"Yeah, I'll let you know, I'm sure it will be good. You know, maybe I could do that."
Mom's face became a blank waiting for a new expression. I had wrapped the handles of the plastic bag so tightly

around my fingers half an hour later there would still be red marks on my skin.

"Be a delivery driver…"

"I knew what you meant."

Anger? Was she angry at me?

"Driving can be dangerous, the roads are crazy; your Dad nearly got in a wreck yesterday."

Hopefully he hadn't been drinking. I mean, he probably *had* been but hopefully not *a lot*. If he had ended up in jail my Mom would have become even more of a mess. I wanted to point out that people get shot up in offices, too, but that seemed cruel.

"It was a stupid idea…"

She touched my arm and it hurt because I knew it was only for a moment. My Mom touched me and then pulled away like I was an electrical socket she had stuck a fork in. It was like I was the ghost of someone she loved and would give anything to see again but the ghost isn't enough: Ghosts are cold. Ghosts move things from their rightful places.

"Have you thought about online college courses?"

I was no longer looking in her eyes but instead focusing on the feeling of the plastic cutting into my fingers, the weight of food as it swung slowly--

"Yeah, maybe I'll check out some after I eat."

And then I was drifting through my door. My mother didn't follow, didn't bother with any more words. The hand that touched me was gone and maybe her heart was as well.

# 9

My old high school had closed by the night of the slowly swinging plastic bag. The students who were left would be starting the next year at different schools. We used to have five high schools in my old town, by the time I graduated there was one.

No one knows why our teacher shot us because he used his last bullet on himself. Maybe he was angry because we were not paying attention to him, just messing around like stupid kids. Someone told me that Jacob had been pranking the teacher and there was another rumor that the teacher had a crush on a girl--maybe R--and it had gotten to him. We'll never know the reason because the brain that made the gun come out ended up on the same dirty tile as my blood and R's and several other students. I remember the teacher's face looking even more like a sad moon if sad moons could sweat. I remember words coming out as if they were on tight sharp springs--
Did he want people to know his name--lots of people? A number you can only reach when you do something amazing or amazingly bad?
I don't think the teacher shot us to become famous. I mean, if that was the case why would he kill himself before he could enjoy the fame?
That made no sense.

*Maybe you can only start to live when you stop thinking.*

I haven't thought about this in years but tonight is a night
to think about it, I guess--
*Time to get your business in order*--did the man at the front
of the room say that?
R was reading, she could read really well before the coma.
I remember her voice bouncing off the hard surface of her
desk and then Jacob saying something before running
towards the door. Someone else saw what he saw and was
trying to run but Jacob grabbed him and--
Pop. Poppoppoppop but loud, louder than you can imagine
things being loud.
Jacob tried to use a kid as a shield but the kid was short and
the bullet went over his head and into Jacob's--
I didn't see it happen, I was watching the moon.
The moon was no longer a sad moon, it was a stern moon,
a thinking moon--
And then I got punched. No, I got shot and it hurt but the
hurt was distracted by the sound of my best friend
shrieking because *she* got shot.
And then I was watching the moon explode--it was that
fast. Not one to two seconds like the Drip, but fast. I could
have kept standing up, my legs were still good, but it felt
right to lie down.
Lying down seemed like the best idea in the world.
My stomach didn't hurt but it felt heavy and numb like a
novacaine mouth. The only pain was in my right hand, it
felt like bees were stinging my fingers--lots of bees; it was
such a distinct feeling that I started to brush them off but
worried my other hand would get stung--

So...I lay on that dirty tile in R's blood and that of a couple of students I didn't really know. More and more every second. Blood. Students. The room no longer smelled like soap and cologne and whatever the janitors cleaned the floor with badly, it smelled like blood and gunsmoke--and the moon was gone. Was it a minute or five minutes? I will never know. The kids who hadn't gotten shot or had only little wounds and were feeling or being brave were going around to us, trying to provide comfort. Some did it well but some had no comfort left to give. Jacob had been shot in the eye. The eye was gone, there was just a hole like a bomb crater--

A bomb crater with a drip, thick sauce down the side like lava from a volcano.

I see it now, I am letting the memory in and remembering how it felt trying to be brave and failing. Some memories light the lost roads you find yourself on like the full moon, some leap from the darkness to remind you of the pain you felt in another life.

# Golden Bullet

# Monday

Dakota Barnes got lucky when that nut shot her and the others at that mortgage company. She gets to go on the interview shows and tell her story. I never get to tell my story. I'd have no problem getting shot if it meant I got on TV. I know it hurts, see it every week on *Folkz Die*, but I don't care. You get in the middle of a high profile shooting and news people talk to you; they ask you questions and let you tell your story. Doesn't matter if you're a stupid bitch like Dakota Barnes, they still want to hear your story.

*Folkz Die* better not be an old show tomorrow. Last week was a repeat but I didn't mind because it was a dope episode. This mean old man got capped with a shotgun. He was yellin' at this other old dude who grabbed his gauge and fired. There's this total spray out the back of the mean old man; seriously, the pellets or whatever just went right through him. He just stood there for a second and then folded at the waist like he was tying his shoe or something. I love it when you get a folder; it's all dramatic and shit. Poetic even.

Dakota Barnes is on *Loud Tawk*. She'll probably go on and on about how it hurts to shit now and everyone will feel sorry for that stupid bitch. Why did she win? Why did she get the Golden Bullet? I've been going for my Golden Bullet for four years now but ain't got nothing.

No one likes their job where I work. People pretend to, but I know better. You can see the smiles they wear peeling at the edges. I was put there by the Agency four years ago and don't make no fuss so they haven't fired me or laid me off or whatever. I act friendly; when people sell shit for their kids I buy some even if all of it's crap.

I almost had a Golden Bullet two years ago with Mike. He had the Happy Face going on, lots of smiles and the Chum Voice, but I could feel his seethe. There was this grimness in his eyes, hate even. When he laughed I could smell the death rolling from inside him. Maybe he just needed gum.

I thought Mike would give me my Golden Bullet. It was so clear to me I had a dream where he walked into work with two Glock 9mms and six extra clips in a black backpack. He asked people if they caught the game or if their loved ones had recovered from illnesses while capping asses and smiling that big ass smile of his. That dream made me happy and I felt hopeful for the first time in years: Maybe I'd get my Golden Bullet then I could tell my story just like Dakota Barnes.

First, I had to nudge Mike closer to the bad place. To do that, you have to isolate someone. I started a rumor that he had given a high school boy crabs. I left a box of those little lice combs next to his cube in a way that looked like he had dropped them. A few days after that I gave a friend's son who goes to a local high school five dollars to wave at Mike's car when he left work. The kid waved. He even scratched the front of his pants like he had crabs or something. Mike didn't wave back, but lots of people saw the high school boy waving.

Less people talked to Mike. He seemed angry a lot of the time and his smiles became less frequent. I popped one of his tires on his car and put a dent in one of the doors--he would no longer live in a dent free world. When Mike went out to his car that day, I watched from the window and saw him mouth a swear as his face turned red. That made me smile; I was on my way to a Golden Bullet.

That night I got the flu for reals. I knew Mike was close and didn't want to call in but I had the shits hella bad. That was the day Mike came to work and shot eight people. He capped this two-faced bitch Brenda Gooten in the thigh and she got to tell her story on *Big Boom Time*. I was hella pissed off that I missed my Golden Bullet after all my work.

Corporate closed the office for two days while they put on sad faces and people in coveralls cleaned up the blood and flesh and stuff off the fabric walls and carpet. They must have done a shitty job because it smelled like rotting meat and spoiled milk until all the blood and stuff dried, turned to dust, and floated through the office and the vents into our open water bottles and coffee cups. Now they're just black spots and new temps lean against them and walk over them not knowing what they are.

We have a guard who strolls around the lot at work but he's too fat to stop crimes. He's as big as this bro who got popped on *Folkz Die* last month; one bullet totally hit his guts and there was this yellow spray. I think it was fat but some dude on the *Folkz Die* board said it was his liver exploding. Whatever--it was hella cool.

*Loud Tawk* was pretty swank today. They totally made fun of Dakota Barnes and that stupid bitch totally didn't get it. She just kept talking about her movie deal and stuff. Why does that bitch get to tell her story anyway? Why did she get the Golden Bullet? Everyone on the Golden Bullet board hates that ho. We call her lipstick shade Dirty Dakota Red and stuff like that.

Most people on the GB board are cool enough, not too many looz'rz. Awhile back there was this dude named Pablo. We all called him Pablo the Plotter because of all his big talk and ideas. He was cool with it, even signed into rooms as PTP. PTP's big thing was to completely engineer a GB situation; get a bunch of us on the GB board to staff an office and one of us would be the shooter. PTP told us over and over that it was "hella win win": The shooter could totally practice and shoot you where it wouldn't cripple you or kill you or anything like that. Who would be the shooter, though? All of us asked that question. The shooter would have to die or like go to prison for reals--that sux, no one wants that game. PTP was totally into the idea, though. One day maybe five months ago he disappeared from the board. Wonder where he is now?

All of us on the board are working towards Golden Bullets. We're all cool with each other but don't usually share tips; you share a good tip and someone might get a GB before you and get on the shows like *Loud Tawk* or *Big Boom Time* or *Hollah Hour*. I like *Hollah Hour*. Murder Mike is like hella funny; he's a fave on the GB board. Jonah, this dude in Wisconsin who got a GB that severed his spine, got to meet Murder Mike and said he's totally cool for reals. There was this 'ho Bethany that was totally obsessed with him but when her GB came in, it was a head shot and killed her. She got on *Folkz Die*, though, so that's something. Didn't get to tell her story, but got on the TV.

One of my roommates pulled *Shrek 11* off line. Someone on the GB board said it's better than *Shrek 10* so maybe I'll check it out if I have nothing else to do. *UR D' 1* is on, but I'm hella sick of that show. It's supposed to be about normal people who do outrageous stuff for rich people but it sucks now. Last season was cool, this bro ate poop after this rich dude offered him a hundred bucks to do it. It was dope; he still had shit around his mouth when he was talking about it in the confession booth. I think that pissed people off because there's nothing cool like that this season so maybe I'll check *Shrek 11* out.

# Tuesday

The car is broke. I went down to start it but there was just this whirring noise. It started making this scraping noise about two weeks ago and it got worse and worse. Today it is broke for reals. I got some duct tape but I don't think I can fix it. This sux--I was tot'ly late for work and had to walk like eight blocks to where the bus stops. The bus always seems to be full of dirty crazy people. The worst are war vets because they're trained to kill and shit. They get crazy and they can snuff you for reals; I saw some shit like that on *Folkz Die* one time. This vet bro was all screaming about the Haj and shit like that and then he grabbed this big woman with a Valu-Place shopping bag and snapped her neck for reals. She did a tot'l fold, it was hella sick. This cop put like six or seven rounds in the vet. His face got small and then he stumbled back and fell. As he lay on the ground his legs kept moving in slow motion. Someone on the FzD board said it looked like he was riding an invisible bicycle and that tot'ly nailed it: The dying vet looked like he was riding an invisible bicycle.

Cecila had to watch her kids today so I got the cube to myself which is sweet. When she's there our chairs hella bump and stuff.  Plus, she's got all these pix and ceramic things and reeks of nasty perfume. When I make my next shooter I hope he or she will cap Cecila. That may sound fucked up but it would be hella sweet to have a cube to myself. Of course, if she did get capped or left because she was having another kid they'd just shove another temp in here with me. We have two shifts so there are four people's shit in here. You're supposed to not have too much stuff but no one pays attention to that rule.

I get some shit on the GB board because I haven't gotten a Golden Bullet yet after four years. I get called a Tourist but at least half of us are Tourists so I don't feel too bad. Most people get bored or move on after a couple of years so I get some propz for being for reals. They read my blog and see I am totally serious; things just didn't pan. Maybe a third of the people on the board have gotten Golden Bullets. Sometimes it pans for reals but sometimes it's a shooting that doesn't click national and you don't get to tell your story or go on the shows. When it clicks most of the people go through some weird head shit after getting shot and turn on the board. A few stay on, though and they're GB4Rz (Golden Bullet 4 Realz). The main rule is you can't act too big because you got your GB. Maybe half the GB4Rz are there for the board and are hella cool. Murder Mike on *Hollah Hour* is a GB4Rz, he just keeps it on th' d-low so he don't get busted. He's always cool, not getting too big or thinking he's hot shit. About the half the Gb4Rz are bitch-ass, though. They act like stars, all big and doing all this hollah about Tourist-this and Tourist-that. They get flamed until they crawl off with their tail between their legs.

I read up on this shit and found out the odds are low for getting capped at work. You read about it every day but that's like one or two offices out of millions; this is why it is so hard to get your GB. Rarez hell is getting two Golden Bullets. The rarest of all is getting two GBs and surviving like GB Sheila did. She is the total star of the Board. First time it panned she got a head shot that actually grazed her brain. It's hella crazy--she knows this cop who took pictures of the crime scene. Sheila posted them and they're hella nasty with all this blood and bits of brain on the wall. I have to wonder what she thinks when she sees those pictures now and sees the little pieces of meat that used to be in her skull. I guess her brain wasn't broken cause she still blogs.

Unfortunately for Sheila that shooting didn't click, it was just a blip on the local news. Sheila didn't get to tell her story the first time. A few months passed and she was working at another telemarketing company. Phone bank is a high reward GB game for reals: Total stress, total pressure, all rude folkz and mean bosses. I hate phone banks so I can't play it like that. Sheila can and started engineering a shooter. She's hot, so she totally set this guy up and cheated on him with another bro on the bank. A few days after the guy she cheated on found out he came in and shot hella folks. Sheila took two rounds: One jacked up her liver and the other hit her in the leg. It hit her femoral artery and she nearly bled out but it was worth it cause they were tot'l Golden Bullets. She got on all the shows: *Loud Tawk, Holla Hour, Big Boom Time* and even got a mention on *Folkz Die*. Sheila total jackpot'd. Some music dude even made this song with her rapping called Lead Girl; the video was hella sick, had her dancing and shit in this fake office with dancers getting capped. It was dope; shoulda won an award or something.

Despite being on all the shows and shit Sheila is pretty cool. I was in on a chat with her and she was like tot'ly normal. She's going for her third GB which is insane for reals. The odds are 'bout the same as flapping your arms and flying like a bird but she's hardcore. If one person could get a third GB, it's GB Sheila.

Today started off bad but got better. We got a new temp in our department. His name is Scott and I think he has potential. He came in like all temps, nervous and forced smiles, but there's something else going on with him. He smells funny, not bad like a wino, but musky like an animal or something. They plopped him in my cube as all the other ones were full. You know the temp deal: You show up, no one knows anything about you so they plop you in a cube to cool your heels. After awhile, someone shows up with some work, explains it badly, and scurries off. Later, if you're lucky, IT shows up and you get on a computer. It was like that with Scott. He just sat there and I could feel his nervousness getting bigger. It was hella suck; bumping chairs with this nervous guy who smelled like an animal. I got him talking and what I got is that he was in the Army in the Middle East a couple of years ago and when he got out they put him in a hospital. Scott didn't come out and say it but it sounded like a mental hospital. I got him on line so he could check his mail while he cooled his heels. By doing that, though, I may have fucked myself: If I can make Scott lead spray the office he might think I'm his buddy and spare me; no GB for me. I mean, if there's time, I could tot'ly turn on him like a bad lunch, make him hate me, but it may not work out. Also, Army dudes--(and especially Marines)--are a bad bet cause they know how to shoot. It's all over the board: Don't engineer a military person to be the shooter because they know what they're doing and get lots of head shots in. Head shot means dead time and no one hears your story.

The bus home was tot'ly rank. Some old man was farting and this kid kept bumping his pack into me. I wanted to watch a movie on my phone but was sure someone would try and swipe it. Phone is hella sweet, got it last month. It's a Shade Bump. I already had the phone implant last year, tot'ly saved for like a year to get it, just had to buy the screen shades. It's hella sweet for reals; it looks like you're just wearing shades but you can check out movies and shit. I just sweat wearing that shit on the bus because they're always scammers out there who can spot things like Shades. They're right in your grill, pulling the Shades off you and booking. They were like four-hundred for reals; that's a lot of paper.

We have a three bedroom condo with a separate dining room that we partitioned to be another bedroom. Last week the roomies learned Cheyenne is pregnant and is moving back with her moms in another part of the state. The three of us have to find a new roommate, maybe a couple since

Cheyenne has the big bedroom with its own bathroom. She was going to have her boyfriend move in but he kicked her to th' curb so she got all sad and shit and begged her moms to let her live with her 'til she pops her kid out. That leaves the rest of us doing the roommate scramble. Sux.

I've been here two years now. Part of the reason I was cool with so many roomies was that I needed to save up for my implant phone; that was a grip for reals. I have shitty insurance through work that don't cover no implant phone which sux. Since I got the phone I was thinking of maybe looking for a place with only one roommate but now that the car's broke that isn't happening. Work don't pay for shit so it'll take a long time to save the money to move.

*USA Save Me!* was pretty cool this week. This old lady was hella sick and needed a kidney transplant so they brought out five potential donors. Unfortunately, the sick lady picked the Runner, the one who says they'll give you an organ but then gets cold feet. The old lady got a second guess and picked the Donor but died before the operation; her kidneys stopped or something. It's a hella messed up show but interesting. You make the wrong decision and it costs you time which costs your life. I think it's a smart show, too; *Big Boom Time* is just a bunch of people shouting and fronting and laying out smack but *USA Save Me!* is all dramatic and shit.

I got a total buzz on the GB board so I feel good and even forgot about that jacked up car of mine. I figured out how you could get a GB with a shooter who was in the Army: You hobble him or her, make sure their shooting arm is crippled or something. That got me lots of props on the board and I felt good. Watch--next month someone will use my tip to get a GB and I'll still be a Tourist next year. I hope that if that happens I will at least get a shout out.

# Wednesday

Got laid--whatever. It'd been a long time so I made it happen. Hadn't been missing anything. It was just like dropping bricks off an overpass; looking for a thrill, looking to feel alive, but only seeing how hella alone you are.

Went to Boom last night and kicked it with my friends. The DJ was good, played "Footy Footy Gooby Gone" three times. That is a hella tight jam for reals; it's blowing up all over. Median Boyz are the best thing on the radio. I got them all over my phone. I thought about making "Footy Footy Gooby Gone" my 'tone, but that'd be tot'l clown for reals cause everyone got that song as a tone.

Took a taxi home in the middle of the night. The driver was some Arab bro with a big ass mustache listening to some Whitney Houston shit. He kept looking up at the overpasses as we went under them. I was looking up too.

# Thursday

Stupid ass landlord showed up at our door and bitched me out because my car has been sitting in someone else's spot for five days. Move your car! Don't you think I'd be moving it if I could? Believe me; I'd rather be driving around in my beat ass car than being stuck on that bus with crazy homeless people and stinky old men. That dickhead landlord told me I have until next Monday to do something about it.

This place sux. You hear hella people arguing and kids screaming and bros rolling through with the bass way up in the middle of the night. I grew up way out in the sticks. The nearest town was like three miles away and it was hella tiny and shut down by six pm. When I was a kid it sucked big time cause there was hella nothing to do. Now I kind of miss it. Sometimes you just want quiet.

*Loud Tawk* was stupid today. It's always stupid but sometimes it's kinda cool--not today. One of the dudes who sent in a clip was using a power drill to put holes in some boards. He was wearing a blindfold and totally drilled into his hand. Dude started hella screaming these swears and there was all this blood. It was kinda cool, I guess. They do shit like that on LT. They have this regular segment called *Life Hurtz* where people fall down and get in car wreaks and the audience votes on it. The winning clip moves on to the voting for the next day when a new clip is introduced. The champion for the past six days has been Motorcycle Pete. The clip is hella sick; this dude like wipes out for reals on his motorcycle and his arm is torn off. You tot'ly see this arm lying in the middle of the road and Pete sprawled on the pavement a few feet away. He's not moving much, just kinda riding an invisible bicycle like that vet who got shot on the bus. Everyone thought the arm was the only thing wrong with Motorcycle Pete but I guess he got all busted up inside because he died of internal bleeding or some shit like that. It sux his dying like that but at least his story got told. *Loud Tawk* has been interviewing his bros and his family and his girl and all that. Motorcycle Pete is a celebrity for reals; all the talk on the GB board today has been about him. What's going to happen to the loot he gets from the clip? If you make it two weeks you win $10,000 and your clip is retired to some sort of hall of fame or some shit like that. Who gets that $10,000? His girl? His family? It turns out his life kind of sucked. He was in the Army stationed in the Middle East for a couple of years. He didn't get shot or blown up or anything like that but he had some head shit going on. This wasn't on the *Loud Tawk* site, they don't go deep like that, I heard this from some chick on the GB board who was like a friend of a friend. She told us that Motorcycle Pete kept getting fired because he was all messed up in the head from seeing people getting killed and shit. He'd tell his girl he was going to look for work or go on a temp assignment but he'd just be out riding his motorcycle. Sometimes he'd rob a store or something to get some money and that made him even more fucked up. Could be a lot of talk, could be for reals, who knows.

# Friday

One of my roommates has a brother with a huge truck. I can't stand the guy, he's like this total redneck bro with a mustache. I tot'ly did not want deal with his cracker ass but I was getting all this smack from my roommates because the landlord was hassling all of us about my stupid ass car. So I had to do all this nice talk with this redneck so he would show up with his huge truck and all these ropes. He's like hella racist and shit and was talking all this crazy End Times and Jesus talk. My roommate is the same way which is why I usually stay locked in my room or go out to Boom or whatever. She and her brother were talking a lot of weird Jesus shit as my car was being tied to this stupid Hee Haw truck. I had to be in my car to brake and steer and this crazy ass redneck was driving hella fast and I thought I was going to die for reals all because of my stupid ass inbred roommate. We got to this garage and I had to totally pretend to be thankful when I really wanted to smack this guy for driving like an inbred hillbilly and saying all this fucked up shit about things his ignorant ass knows nothing about.

Turns out the starter is broke. Other shit is wrong with my piece of junk car but the starter is the only thing keeping it from running. The tires are bald, but I will seriously drive on bald ass tires because I want out of that apartment and have to save a grip of money to make that happen.

# Monday

We have a room where all the xtra crap is kept at work. I call it the Ghostroom cause there's not much light and it's kinda creepy. It's where I chill out when I need time to myself. I pretend I'm back there looking for an organizer or stapler or something not that I think anyone gives a shit. Cecilia is nice enough but she gets on my nerves for reals. She's always going on about her kids or some beef with her family--talk talk talk talk talk. After a couple of hours of that I need a break and slip back to the Ghostroom to just chill for a few and watch some clips on my shades or some shit like that. I was in there this morning, just chilling in my favorite corner and checking out the boards on my phone when I heard the door open. I slipped my shades into my pocket and bent down so it'd look like I was searching for a new red stapler or some jive like that. This woman was just standing there in the doorway and staring across the room. Was she looking for me? Before I could say something she started saying all these swears and really evil shit, just hissing out the words like a pissed off snake. The woman looked borderline like she was about to go back to her desk, pull out a piece, and hella start capping fools. If she found me, I'd be the first one to get my Golden Bullet. Maybe I should have stood up and yelled "Yo, crackpot!"
Before I could she turned around and walked out.

I got back to my desk with a couple of pads of Post-Its. I already have hella Post-Its but didn't want to come back empty-handed. There was a new Buckaroo Bulletin in my email. For some reason, one of the managers calls office wide email alerts Buckaroo Bulletins. There's even a little cowboy that looks like the Twinkies mascot right down to the lariat and tot'ly insane looking grin. It's probably why I had this hella creepy dream a few months ago where the Twinkie cowboy was chasing my ass. This Buckaroo Bulletin was about a meeting we all had to go to about office behavior or some shit like that.

The meeting was in the break room. It sucked because someone had cooked something nasty in there for lunch. The manager who talked to us kept smiling at weird times and had some sort of skin disease that looked like a really bad rash. He did a whole lot of talk about how management felt we weren't being friendly enough to each other and had hired someone to coach us on being nice or some shit like that. Rash Man did some blah blah blah for what felt like a week and then introduced this woman I hadn't noticed sitting a few seats down from me. She was around fifty, heavy set, and had this dyed brown beehive hairdo. My blood went cold when I recognized her as the lady who had been saying all that crazy shit in the Ghostroom. As she did her blah blah blah she was wearing this huge fake ass smile that went nowhere near her eyes. I wondered how long she would be in our office but didn't ask because it could have been taken the wrong way. I wanted to know because I could see it would take very little work to get a Golden Bullet out of her.

The lady's name was Abby. Some guys at work have already nicknamed her Abby Normal. Abby Normal played some gay ass films showing us the right and wrong ways to act around the office. After the clips Abby went into all this jive about how it takes less muscles to smile than frown and how once you train yourself to just smile when you see people it comes naturally. All the while she had this spooky ass grin plastered across her mug; it was hella fake and everyone knew it. Even though we thought Abby Normal was hella gay we did the smile and nod game to keep the manager off our asses. Who knows if that skin shit he has is contagious.

I walked up to Abby to introduce myself and casually ask how long it usually takes for her to work with an office like ours. The question seemed to confuse her and maybe piss her off a little. I could see it in her eyes that when she pulled the Glock or whatever out of her cheap ass bag that I would be the first to get capped.
That time I smiled for real--it was gonna be a good day.

Abby Normal had no idea how long she would be in office, maybe a few weeks.
A few weeks would be more than enough time.

# Tuesday

*Golden Bullet Board is a fake. Got it? Golden Bullet Board is hella fake!*
That's what I told 'em. That's what all of us tell 'em: GB is just a joke; tot'ly clownin for reals.

I knew what was up when I got the email: Please report to such and such place at such and such time by order of United States Homeland Security. The Feds had been watching us. The Feds obviously thought we were bad guys.

I had my beat ass car back in time for the appointment and drove out to the industrial part of town. The address was a warehouse. It seemed weird but it's the Feds so what can you do? The door was guarded by these two huge Blackwater bros with machine guns. They were all scowling and looking hard. I asked one if I was at the right place.
"Yep, step inside."
The warehouse was one big room. At each corner was a Blackwater guy with cheap sunglasses and a machine gun. These guys had suits unlike the outside guys who were in black t-shirts and black cargo pants. At one end of the room there was a stage with a hella big poster of President Reagan behind it. Facing the stage were a few dozen folding metal chairs, most of them already taken. This woman walked up to me; she had tha bump on da left

implant phone and was wearing a big fake ass smile. She asked my name and when I told her and she repeated it into her phone. I guess that's how they registered us. I took one of the seats and a voice came over the PA speakers to say that everything would be starting in a couple of minutes.

I already knew what was going to happen; it was all over the Board. The two minutes we were cooling our heels I was all nerves for reals. A middle-aged joker with a cheap dye job and a blue suit walked down the middle aisle as some old ass rock song played over the PA. He jumped on stage and the music faded as he walked up to the microphone with a big car sales grin.
"How's everybody doin'?!"
His voice was big and happy but his eyes were dead looking. Dye Job gave us his blah blah blah about how after 9-11 America has to keep things hella tight security wise to keep bad people from stealing freedom and shit. He also explained how Homeland Security is here to protect our liberties and freedoms. After his spiel, Dye Job explained why we were there: All of us had been hanging out on-line with potential terrorists and had taken part in talk that could be seen as promoting terrorism in the United States.
Shit like that makes your blood go cold for reals: Homeland Security thinks I'm a terrorist.
Dye job reassured us that they didn't see us as dangerous because if they did we'd be in jail. No, he told us, HS just wanted to help us consider the direction we are taking our lives in. Ten minutes later, we were allowed to leave.

Driving home I felt hella sick to my stomach: The GB Board is my life. My job is shit, my car is shit, and I live with a buncha clowns--the Board keeps me going. I'm down with GB 4 realz. But, if I keep being GB 4 realz some Blackwater clowns could throw me in a van and lock me up without a trail.
That's some hardcore shit.
What was I gonna do?

I needed booze--I needed to get seriously jacked up on gin and tonics so I stopped at Valu-Place on the way home. Looking for the booze aisle I ran into Abby Normal. She had one of her crazy ass smiles plastered on her mug as she pushed her cart along. Looking in it I saw a blowtorch, pliers, an electric sander, and a grip of industrial strength garbage bags.
"You're not smiling," she nodded at me.
I forced a smile so big it made my nostrils hurt.
"Sorry, Abby, still on working on it."
She just nodded and kept pushing her shopping cart full of stuff towards check-out.

# Wednesday

They're in pre-production on the Dakota Barnes movie. It's only a Net movie and IMDB says it's only going to be about thirty minutes long but she still gets to tell her story. I think people are finally getting sick of her and her hot mess cause they were tot'ly making fun of her on *Loud Tawk* this morning. One of the guys did her voice dead on, tot'ly whining like Dakota whines--it was hella funny. "Dakota" was going on and on about how it's hard for her to poop just like Dakota's blah blah blah in real life. *Loud Tawk* was hella in Dakota's corner after she got out of the hospital but I guess they got sick of her just as all of us got sick of her.

After eight days Motorcycle Pete finally lost to a new clip on *Life Hurtz*. This one has an accident where two buddies are cutting down trees and one chainsaws the other's arm off; it's some nasty ass shit. The camera is right on the guy who loses his arm and there's hella blood spray and the arm just hangs for a second on some meat or something before dropping off. This dude is tot'ly watching his arm hang there and you can see the disappointment on his face as the meat or whatever it is breaks and the arm hits the ground. Maybe he was worried about it getting dirty. They can sew that shit back on but if it gets dirty that's bad news.

I am tot'ly getting hooked on the *Life Hurtz* board. Most people just want to talk about LH with other people into the show.  But, like any board, there's some haters and some flamers and shit like that. There's one hater who is all "*Life Hurtz* is fake, some of those clips are totally shot, totally scripted; you can tell they're using lighting and mics." Blah blah blah. Later he was doling out all this smack about the winning clip: "Why were two buddies out cutting trees with another buddy filming them?" Who knows? Maybe one of them got a new camera or something and wanted to try it out. Haters. I know some of them wanted Motorcycle Pete to win: Motorcycle Pete had a hard time for reals and it's hella cool they were going to donate the winning money to a charity that helps veterans with head shit, but he had eight days—

He just wasn't good enough to win; Chainsaw Dude kicked him to the curb.

I couldn't stay away from the GB board.  I did a post and it was tot'ly about how Homeland Security called me down: "HS thought I was a terrorist for reals; they don't know we a buncha jokers."

I got all these responses laughing with me:

"Yeah, they don't know we hella make these stories up. GB is not for reals, not for reals at all."

Of course, it *is* for real, I mean, everything I've posted is hella for reals and if the shit the others put up ain't real they deserve a writing prize or something.

I finally broke down and put "Footy Footy Gooby Gone" on as one of my ringtones; that jam is hella sick.

# Thursday

I tot'ly had to call in sick today; life is tot'ly fucked up for reals.

We found out last night that GB Sheila is a fake; she tot'ly shot all those people in that office and framed the person everyone thought was the shooter. Sheila was worried she wouldn't get her second GB so she set it all up.

What the fuck do you do with that? I had "Lead Girl" for one of my ringtones! I used to watch that clip over and over I mean--

Sheila was my girl, know what I'm sayin'?

She tot'ly set the bar and now--

I don't know how to say the shit that's on my mind; it's like a movie without words. We hella thought Sheila was GB4Rz; we thought she'd be the one who could get a third GB odds or no odds.

What if there are other fakers on the Board? What if they're all fakers? This has tot'ly been my life for years. What the fuck is real?

I just kept saying that to myself this morning: *What the fuck is real?*

I couldn't even bring the Board up this morning. It reminded me of what it's like when you have a bad break-up and avoid going where you think the other person is gonna be.

I didn't eat all morning, just hung out on the *Life Hurtz* board. More haters had started threads pointing out why the chainsaw clip is fake. The thing they all blah blah blah'd about was the fact those bros were filming themselves cutting down trees. The more I hung out on the LH board the more I missed the GB board--*my* board. The more time I spent there the more it seemed that the LB board was a bunch of tourists. No one seemed to feel LH the way we feel GB stuff on our board; it seemed like just a way for a bunch of fools to kill time.

After a few hours I brought up the GB Board. There were hella posts about Sheila: Why? What was up with that bitch? It felt good, you know? Everyone on that board--my board-- tot'ly felt the same as me. Lead girl my ass. Yeah, we had one tot'l fake, wha-ev, but the rest of us are GB4Rz.

# Friday

This sux. OMG, this tot'ly sux 4 reals.

I was running hella late this morning. Beat ass car, it still isn't working right. But B4 that--

B4 that, crazy Jesus roommate had the shits 4 reals so I had no bathroom to get ready in. I finally got in, did my stuff, and ran out to my beat ass car. I turn the key and it makes that same noise it made B4 I spend a grip on getting it "fixed." Fucking mechanics; all hella liars. Finally got it started and tot'ly drove faster than I shoulda in that shitty car and got to work hella late. U know the drill: Run to your cube and start working hoping no one notices how late U R.


Abby Normal was wandering around, making sure we were all smiling and being nice. She was whacking this shiny metal ruler on the edge of our cubicles as she smiled that spooky ass grin of hers, looking like a ghoul or some shit like that. I imagined that ruler replaced with a Glock or an electric sander or a nail gun. Right before she cut me down she'd say in that syrupy voice of hers: "One last smile, buckaroos! One last smile!"

I'd bet hella money she puts that shiny ruler in her private area and gets really angry and breaks up stuff in her cheesy apartment when it doesn't bring the right feelings.

Fuck, sux sux sux! I didn't *know*—I guess you can't know what this kinda shit is gonna be like--

K gotta focus, gotta tell my story like I'm on *Holla Hour* or *Loud Tawk* or *Big Boom Time*. I've been shooting some footage; the light isn't so good in here and I have to whisper--

A couple of hours went by and I was doing my work, nose down 4 reals. Supervisor hadn't said anything, hadn't IMd me or nothing so I thought I was in the clear. Ceceila was farting up a storm and it was so strong I could almost taste it. At the same time I was taking notes on my phone just like I'm doing now, planning the coming weeks and setting up Abby to be a shooter cause she was so obvious and then--
U remember a couple weeks back when I had that ex-military guy in our cube? I guess something bad went down 4 him because he's back. First thing he did was cap the rent-a-cop out in the parking lot. I heard the shot and ran over to the window. I saw the rent-a-cop's legs--just his legs--so I have no idea where he was hit. His legs were still, not riding an invisible bike or nothing, so I am guessing he's dead. It was weird because I didn't feel scared or anything; it felt like I was in a movie, the hero of a movie even.

Everyone knew what was going on and were looking towards the front doors. A few moments later the shooter came walking up with an automatic in his hand, some 9mm piece. He was wearing shades and his face was as flat and blank as the asphalt the rent-a-cop was lying on. Some people freaked and just ran around aimlessly. Some people froze where they stood and just watched the crazy dude come on. A few were smart and headed for the back door. It's supposed to sound an alarm when you open it but the alarm has been broke since the last shooting. I found a good way to frame the shooter and started filming him. I looked across the room and saw some chick doing the same thing. She saw me and nodded so I nodded back. Maybe they'll have us both on *Loud Tawk* at the same time; they've never done that before but who knows. The shooter used the rent-a-cop's badge to get in. He saw us watching him and smiled this smile that was way scarier than any grin that had ever crossed Abby Normal's mug.

"You thought it'd be me, didn't you?"

I looked over and saw Abby crouching next to a cubicle. She looked scared and for the first time was not smiling. Seeing her not smiling made it all real and I started feeling really scared myself.

The shooter started picking people off. He was not wild or random; he took his time and made each round count. The manager with nasty rash got it in the head and there was this spray of head shit and skin flakes. I could smell the gunpowder and the gore and the way he fell I could see that like half of his skull was missing. I powered through my fear by imagining Murder Mike watching me intently on *Holla Hour* as I told my story. I focused on that as I kept filming the crazy dude as he nailed Pha from marketing in the back. She cried out like she was having an orgasm and sprawled in the corridor to the exit. The shooter was only about twenty feet from me at that point. I was hoping

maybe he'd hit me in the shoulder or somewhere else
non-lethal--

You start thinking crazy shit like that, wondering where it
would hurt least to be shot. In the arm? The leg? Leg shots
are tricky cause if it hits the femoral artery you can bleed
out before the parameds show up.

Fuck, why did my shooter have to be a military dude?

And then I got shot.

I was so focused on where it'd hurt least to be shot I didn't
notice the shooter was sighting me. It was fast; one second
I was lost in thought and the next it felt someone was
punching me in the stomach hella hard. After a couple of
seconds there was this burning kind of numbness that burns
4 reals if I move but--

I knew if I stayed there I'd get capped in the head so I
staggered back here to the Ghost Room. It hurts like fuck
shit damn so I am focusing on telling my story to Murder
Mike, just focusing on his face as he listens to me telling
my story. I am tot'ly jacking my keypad up typing
this--blood is making the keys sticky.

Ain't been no shots for a few minutes. I ain't bleeding 2
much; there's blood, but it ain't spray or anything--I'm gut
shot like Dakota Barnes. Maybe I'll have trouble with my
poops. I got my GB, though, just gotta focus on that.

Haven't heard no shots for awhile; maybe it's safe to go
out.

# Epilogue

{conversation on the GB Board a few days later}
GBMMikeFan4: You see the news? TargetD7 got their GB
GB Panther: Yeah, but TargetD7 was stupid; stuck their head out during r-load.
GB Starkweather: U saw my footage. I saw TargetD7 come outta tha closet, motioned for them to stay down, just r-load I whispered.  Target D7 didn't listen, got capped in the head.
GBMMikeFan4: Sux. Target D7 won't be able to tell their story, hella sux. You sell that clip to *Folkz Die*?
GB Starkweather: Someone from *Folkz Die* sent me a msg but they were trying 2 hella low-ball but I ain't playin' that. That shit is worth a grip and maybe a spot on the shows.
GBPanther: But U didn't get a GB, you can't get on the shows!
GB Starkweather: M-be. But this clip is hella dope; I'm gonna get paid 4 realz--iz all bout g-tn paid.

# Coda: Death Becomes Dewy Green

# 1

I didn't see that fight coming. The guys I got into it with looked like wimps: Hipsters with beards and expensive jeans that their girlfriends probably picked out for them. Manpurses. Soft boy talk including a bunch of blahblahblah about some trendy vegan restaurant--
Vegans don't get in bar fights, they watch them in movies. Me? I'm no fighter for a number of reasons.
The beardos were going on and on about Dewy Green. They were drinking this weeks IPA and pricey bourbon while making Dewy Green out to be a fucking saint or something. I got sick of it and told them to shut the fuck up.
One of them turned towards me, he looked stunned and smiled like he was unsure whether I was joking or not.
I wasn't and stared back.
He asked if I was "some kind of asshole or something."
I told him that I was sick of hearing people go on and on about that stupid bitch Dewy Green.
His buddy--who looked even more like a nerd--got a pissed off expression on his hairy face and jumped off his stool. *What the fuck did you say?*
I repeated myself: *I am sick of hearing people go on and on about that stupid bitch Dewy Green.*
And he came at me with a clumsy swing that I almost walked into. I threw an equally awkward punch. A second later people were pulling us apart.

Since I am the regular and they're tourists the bartender
kicked them out.
"You okay, Cobalt?"
"Yeah, can I get another one, please, Kevin?"
"What the fuck did you say to those guys?"
"I told them to shut up about Dewy Green."
Kevin nodded, he knows my story.

# 2

I have been keeping my mouth shut for over two years.
I have been biting my tongue and holding back and I guess
I reached my breaking point.
Dewy Green was no hero.  She was not a stupid bitch--I'm
sorry I said that--but she was no hero. I knew Dewy Green:
We were roommates, we were friends--
Lots of people say that last part, I know that--
I had all sorts of shit on my phone from when Dewy and I
hung out like texts and pics  but I got drunk one night and
erased it all. I don't even remember why I did it; I do stupid
shit like that when I am drinking...like get in fights with
hipsters.

Dewy Green wasn't all bad. The thing is, she wasn't all
good either--she was just a normal person who could be
cool or fucked up like anyone else. The "hero" Dewy
Green didn't exist.  She didn't die whispering for us to
"carry on the revolution" or whatever the beardos think.
Dewy didn't say anything after they shot her, she was too
torn up and just sort of gasped and moaned. You know how
people sound when they're fucking?  It was like that.  She
didn't die in the middle of planning some big political
thing, she just got shot after getting in a stupid beef with a
cop.  I told her to shut up but it didn't do no good.  Dewy
could be really stupid sometimes--would she shut up even
when her life depended on it?  No.

Everything that happened the night Dewy was killed is so clear to me. Normally my memory is shit but every detail from that night is clear as a glass of warm gin. We had just gotten off our Under 20s at the Wal-Mart on 82nd. I was ragging on Dewy as we waited for the bus, calling her "princess" because she only had two Under 20s while I had three. She was being quiet--unusual for her--and I could tell that she was thinking about something.

"No witty comeback, princess?"

"No. Not tonight, Cobalt."

There was a seriousness surrounding her and it made me uncomfortable. Dewy picked up on that and smiled. It was obvious that she didn't feel like smiling and was doing it for my benefit.

"Here's some trivia for you, Cobalt: Why did Under 20s become a thing?"

"Fuck if I know."

"Well, about five years ago they made it so people who worked more than 20 hours a week but less than 40 had rights. The big companies created Under 20s to get around those rights."

"Yeah, I think I remember my dad telling me about that."

She shrugged and looked down the road. There weren't many cars out that late.

"We need to stop at the store on the way home, I need to get some wine."

"Awesome. More Chill River antifreeze for my homegirl."

Normally she would have had some comeback to that but Dewy was just *quiet* as we waited in the cold. A couple of minutes later, our bus came.

The story I heard is that someone matching Dewy's description had been spotted at a protest in the area. A cop spotted Dewy through the window of the bus, ran her biometrics or some shit like that, and stopped the bus. He got on and came back to talk to Dewy and get her ID. 5-0 wasn't being a dick or anything like that, honestly he seemed pretty cool for a cop. It took a lot of cuss words and smack talk from Dewy to set him off. After how quiet she had been her orneriness seemed to come out of nowhere.

Dewy was just looking for a beef; she was pissed off and ready to brawl.

D was angry a lot of the time and sometimes she just needed to vent. Most times she just cussed but a few times she started brawls.

Honestly, I don't know why she hadn't been killed before that night--killed or beat down.

At the Wal-Mart she was always sassin' our boss, always starting shit with him--she didn't care if he was a manager, Jordan was just another douche bag to her. I guess he wanted to fuck Dewy because he never took her job away. It makes no sense but maybe J had a thing for plain girls. Dewy wasn't ugly but she wasn't hot or anything like that. Her hair wasn't that great and she had a hardness to her face. Her tits were pretty nice but other than that she wasn't someone you would think of as hot. She did have her moments where she could be sweet; sometimes she'd buy you a drink if you were in the black or get you some McBell for no reason.

Dewy had a cool side but she could also be a bitch…
It all balanced out, I guess.

I don't even blame the cops for what happened, not even
the one who machine-gunned Dewy. That was just a stupid
accident; he paniced. The only person I still feel anger
toward is the guy who filmed Dewy dying as he bragged
about all the money he was going to get. He told all these
stories about how he was buddies with her, I even heard
that he said that Dewy told him stuff before she died.
No, he just stood there filming her from a safe distance
with his cheap ass phone.
As she bled out he was talking about he was "gonna get
paid" and how he was gonna "get this shit on *Folkz Die*."
*I'm gettin' paid for reals!*
Dewy would be brawling for reals if she knew what a grip
that fool probably made. That video was just the beginning;
I saw a picture of Dewy on a t-shirt with the slogan "Make
some noise!" and almost puked.
Someone got hella rich off some girl they didn't even
know.
Some chick got on *Hollah Hour* because she was one of
the people who saw Dewy get shot. This girl had all this
blahblahblah about how the shooting had fucked with her
head and that she couldn't work anymore.
*I keep having nightmares about Dewy being shot, some
days I'm too scared to leave my house.*
And yet she was together enough to hire a PR company to
get on the shows.

# 3

The first few months I knew Dewy she was just another loud girl that I worked with; we didn't become friends until we lived together. When she became my roommate I'd already been in that condo for years. The condo had originally been three bedrooms but to save money on rent earlier roommates had turned the dining room into another bedroom with some quilts and boards. I started off in that room but after a couple of years a regular bedroom opened up and someone else took my place. My room was haunted when I first moved in, I'd see these weird shadows in the corner and feel like someone was watching me. One roomie told me that the person who had the room a couple of years earlier had died in a workplace shooting. I tried to ask her more about it but M didn't want to talk about it. A girl at work told me to burn some sage; I thought it was a stupid idea but after I did it the strange presence went away and hasn't come back.

Now I'm only haunted by Dewy. Sometimes I think I can smell her shampoo. Sometimes I could swear I see a girl in a big coat walking up to the house and I'll forget--

I'll forget she's dead. I'll run up to the girl only to see it isn't Dewy and then--

It'll all come back to me...her death and how I felt right after it happened.

We had a really hard time renting the quilt and board room. Michelle thought it was because it wasn't a real room but I didn't agree; this town is full of unofficial bedrooms. I told anyone who would listen that I needed a new roommate but Dewy was the only one who seemed interested.

*You still looking for a roomie, Cobalt?*

That girl hounded me for weeks about the room. Eventually I gave in and it changed my life. When I showed Dewy the condo she didn't like the room with the blanket walls. She even had the nerve to tell me that she wanted my room instead. When I told little miss sunshine to fuck off she offered to suck my cock if I'd rent her my bedroom.

*Right, sweetie, yeah--you keep that desperate little mouth to yourself; you ain't gettin' my room.*

After that incident I was worried that Dewy would be a pain in the ass to live with but she wasn't bad. If she had a guy over she could be loud but whatever. The only other beef I had with her was when she got up in my business, telling me to stand up to my parents or shit like that. She'd get all into our family shit and start talking smack about my mom and dad. I had to shut that down a few times, her putting her nose in family stuff. My parents aren't bad people, they're just kind of obtuse: Before I came out they would talk all sorts of smack about fags and queers; not hateful, just stupid. When I came out to them, though, they were cool. I know it wasn't easy for them--

Some parents say *I always knew*, I could tell by my folks' faces they hadn't known or were holding out hope that what they sensed about me would pass or something. When I came out to them my folks looked shocked like something bad had happened right in front of them and they weren't sure how to react--

*We need time, okay, son?*

Son. That was a good sign. I went away and came back a couple of days later. My parents hugged me at the door like they always did. Right away they started suggesting that I try out for one of those reality shows like *Fruity Fabulous!* or *Butt Broz.* It was a ridiculous idea but I saw what they were doing and just smiled and nodded and pretended to agree it was a great idea--

I could see they loved me and were desperate to find a silver lining in the big, gay cloud that had settled over them. I'd still be queer, but at least they could tell all their obtuse friends that their son was famous.

It wouldn't matter if I was famous for sucking cock and fucking boys up the ass, at least I'd be famous.

They've never came out and said that but I know them too well--

I may be stupid but I am not obtuse.

Dewy went on and on about how their acceptance was *conditional* or maybe even delusional. She was always telling me that I should sass my parents more, that I should show up for food with a boy in assless dungarees or something like that.

*Oh, shut up, Dewy!*

I don't know how many times I said those four words to that girl.

Those hipsters didn't know that side of her; hell, maybe they would have even liked her more.

# 4

I had a smart, serious roommate who didn't drink. I couldn't stand her being around, I wanted someone fun who I could drink with and talk to. Dewy was all that. She also drove me nuts with her loud talk and dark moods. That girl was always up for a fight, she could be a real sweetheart but D could turn on a dime.

I think Dewy was so ornery because she *was* smart; this is a shitty world if you're intelligent. D may have been smart but she was also obtuse, always talking about cops and the government around security cameras. I'd try to shush her but she'd always wave me off. Some people would say it was proof that she was a revolutionary but Dewy was just being angry--

Being angry can make you stupid, it can even make you dead.

Some assclowns think Dewy was a Muslim lover because she stood up to that cop. Dewy didn't give a shit about no Muslims, neither of us did. A lot of people I know hate Muslims and think they're all out to kill us or something. Dewy's parents were educated so they taught her about all that Middle East shit like Arabs and Muslims. The only asshole Muslim I've ever known was my boss at Burger King, Madras Mike. I'm pretty sure he was Arab but we called him Madras Mike because it sounded better than Arab Mike. He found out about his nickname. Instead of being pissed off he told us that he liked it and that it would be his stage name. Madras Mike had this lame music recording app on his phone. He would come up with these stupid raps when we were trying to flip burgers or man the fryers. Those stupid ass raps were always about shooting people or pussy or selling drugs. When you listened to the words you could tell that Mike knew nothing about any of those things. When he found out that I'm queer Mike would go on and on about it when he wasn't doing his lame ass raps.

*Hey, Cobalt, you want to see my cock? It's pretty big, I think you'd like it. You know, I am bi-sexual myself...*

What can you do? He's the boss, the man with the plan. All you can do is play up the "flaming queen" bit because you know that is your role to play:

*Oh, I can be fabulous, sweetie!*

It's a role, it's a cartoon--you're expected to be a cartoon like a cartoon monkey in a cartoon jungle.

Dewy understood that but wouldn't play along. More than anyone I have ever known, Dewy did not give a fuck.

# 5

The night Dewy died was so fucked up...
I had never seen someone die right in front of me. I'd seen
shit on *Folkz Die* and the other shows but I'd never seen
anyone smoked from just a few feet away. You'll see
people shoot at each other a block or two away sometimes
but from that distance you don't see blood spraying and you
don't *smell* it. When Dewy was shot I smelled the gun
smoke and all the blood and other shit coming out of her. It
was loud and then it was really quiet even though there
must have been twenty people standing around. No one
was making any noise, not the passengers, not the cops.
The only person talking was that dude with the camera. He
kept saying the same thing over and over like a mantra: *I
am gonna get paid, I am so gonna get paid.*
Everyone else was just staring at Dewy, even the cops.
They had to know that they totally fucked up--
I always wonder if they considered killing the rest of us to
cover things up.
A lot of the witnesses looked dazed: *Did that really
happen?* A couple of them seemed to enjoy it like a good
movie or a video game, I could see it in their eyes.
*I am gonna get paid, I am so gonna get paid.*
That guy filming Dewy dying makes me think of all those
fools who play the lotto like my dad.
"Somebody has to win."
That's what he always says: *Somebody has to win.*

I think it's a way to disconnect from his shitty life, living in the bubble of a stupid dream--
*Somebody has to win.*
Dad has been going on about the lotto for years, I can imagine what sort of fantasies he has:
He'll win the lotto and then my folks will be able to move out of that crappy apartment.
He'll win the lotto and his queer son will become a reality TV star and no one will have to eat frozen burritos again. I always associate frozen burritos with being broke and having no time for real food because you're always rushing to one of your Under 20s.
When you win the lotto I am guessing you don't have to eat frozen burritos.
Dewy didn't play the lotto, I'm pretty sure she thought it was bullshit.
She had no hopes, no dreams, no goals.
Her parents went to college and all it got them was debt; they lived in a shitty apartment just like my parents who never got past high school. Dewy saw college as stupid bullshit, which is how she saw pretty much everything.

# 6

Some people got riled up when Dewy got shot.
Some people thought that things would change but those
people are just like that stupid ass counselor who told me to
stay in school another year.
Everyone knows that shit is fucked up but no one knows
how to fix it.
It's like all my friends with broken cars: They wanted a car
so they bought some old beater that doesn't work because
it's all that they could afford. They don't have the money
to take it to a mechanic and they can't fix it themselves.
Maybe they even *know* what is broken but they don't know
how to fix it--the world is like that. Dewy being killed
woke some people up but most of them went back to sleep.
What are they gonna do--write some angry blog that only
other angry bloggers are gonna read? Protest on the street?
All you get from protesting is a concussion when some cop
busts your head.
Maybe Dewy was smart enough to understand that or
maybe she was just *aware*. Being aware can be worse than
being smart, picking up on all the fucked up shit out there.

I was aware when I was a kid but learned how to tune it
out. I still remember how the teachers taught us by using
copied pages from old textbooks that had fallen apart. We
didn't have no books, just those copied pages. The copier
sucked and would snag all the time and smudge the pages
so it was half readable--no wonder we never learned shit in

those classes. Most of my teachers seemed angry or worn out: One cried all the time. Some reeked of booze or pot. One was so old she'd piss herself and her panty hose had piss stains down the legs. Teaching has to be a fucked up job--

You probably know what's up when you're a teacher, that there's no point in trying to teach anything because most of the kids are just going to get a GED and be working two or three Under 20s. Most jobs have been dumbed down so much even a retard can do them well.

No joke: I've worked with three or four retards--full on retards.

One of them retards even got employee of the month and when they told him he got so excited he pulled this big old boner out of his retard pants.

The boss had no idea what to do. He stopped talking and was making a point not to look at his employee of the month. Eventually he told us to get back to work and that retard put his big ol' dong back in his slacks. Later in the shift, Madras Mike started beatboxing and making up some lame ass rap about Handicap Hard-Ons.

One of the fat girls who runs the register kept talking about the retard's big dick and how she was going to fuck him.

I never found out if she did but I wouldn't be surprised.

*What is there to do but drink and fuck?*

Dewy said that more than once when she was being Fun Dewy, the Dewy Green I like to remember.

If she wanted to fuck a retard with a big dick she would have done it and not given a shit what you thought--

That was how she lived; it was as if she understood that she would die young and it was pointless to worry about what other people thought.

Dewy's getting shot isn't the only fucked up story out there. I knew a guy who worked four Under 20s; he was like 22 and had five kids: He finally lost his shit and killed his whole family. When Dewy died some people thought shit like that would change, that enough people would be pissed off and there would be a revolution or something. It's been two years and there are still people waiting for shit to happen.

It's like my Dad and the lotto; he has spent thousands on scratchers and quik-pix. I think that on some level he knows the odds of winning are crazy low but the dream of winning is all he has--

Maybe the idea of a perfect Dewy Green is all these wanna be revolutionaries have.

My Dad isn't going to win shit and Dewy was just some girl who got pissed off, sassed a cop, and ended up on *Folkz Die.*

Dewy was just a chick who worked at Wal-Mart and this depressing shoe store.

She drank too much cheap wine and fucked lots of guys with goatees and backwards caps and shitty taste in music. Dewy was clueless when it came to men, even had this crazy idea that we should be boyfriend and girlfriend.

*Uh, I ain't wired like that sweetie!*

*You ain't hearin' me, Cobalt. We'll have sex with other people but we'll take care of each other.*

*We already do, Dewy, you've been drinking again.*
But I didn't take care of her, if anything I failed her.

# 7

I didn't want to die.
At some point I realized that a line had been crossed and
Dewy was going to be killed--period--and I could either
stand back and live or die with her.
I couldn't see what Dewy saw or feel what she felt.
I *could* see that the cop was going to get us smoked if we
started a beef with him--why didn't she?
You could feel it, that things were getting out of control--D
*had* to have felt it.
I was trying to talk Dewy down, I was totally *begging* her
to just chill, but she wasn't listening; D just got all weird
and pissed off and red in the face. A couple of other people
tried to talk to her--everyone gave a shit except Dewy.
Even after a second cop got on the bus and started barking
at her she didn't dial it down. I have no idea what was
going on in her head or why she got off that bus--
They won't shoot you on the bus. They might taze you and
you shit yourself and it sucks but you don't die.
No: Dewy got off that bus like a dumbshit and was all
aggro and reaching in her bag and they shot her. 5-0 had
called out some sort of a riot truck with a machine gun
mounted on it. From what I heard the cop on that truck was
pretty much a rookie so he overreacted and fired enough
bullets to nearly cut Dewy in half.

Dewy's family wanted to talk to me. They wanted to know
everything: What our jobs at Wal Mart were like. Who D

dated. They even wanted to know the really gross stuff like what happened when Dewy was shot.

They had to ID her in the morgue so they had to have seen how fucked up she was--

Maybe they wanted to know about the last couple of minutes she was alive.

Those last two minutes where things could have gone differently and D could have lived.

I've thought about that many times.

I thought about it a lot but had to let it go.

My friend is dead and all the stupid fantasies in the world aren't going to change that.

After Dewy was killed her older sister got all up on my jock, she seemed obsessed with me for some reason. I couldn't get with all that and it wasn't just that I'm not into girls, it was more that Pepi was just off the hook and intense or whatever.  She'd text me all the time looking for some meaning in her sister being shot. I told her that I didn't think there *was* any meaning, that it was just a stupid situation that got out of hand. That answer didn't seem to satisfy Pepi. Dewy's sister had some head stuff going on and each time I saw her it seemed to be worse.

I could have switched out my phone but she knew where I lived.

I thought about calling the cops but I felt sorry for her.

Pepi was a hot mess but she wasn't a bad person. In fact, I'm pretty sure she was a good person, just a little insane. She told me that she was writing a book about what happened to Dewy and even sent me some of it. What she wrote was just nuts: She turned Dewy's death into this weird, mixed up story that just reeked of crazy girl.

A few months after Dewy was shot Pepi hooked up with some guy and got pregnant. That was a big relief because it stopped her from trying to be my crazy girlfriend. Her baby daddy got some job in Nebraska or one of those states no one in their right mind lives in. They moved away and that was that.

The situation with Pepi started when her and her parents came to get Dewy's stuff. I had to rent Dewy's room out which meant that I had to get rid of her crap. Taking care of her shit sucked because I had to deal with all those crazy Greens with all their book words and intense gazes. All D had were old clothes and some worthless crap that should have been thrown out but the Greens said they wanted all of her stuff. They were dealing with their daughter and sister being killed and I didn't want to be a dick. It took weeks for the Greens to get all of Dewy's shit because they only had one cardboard box--one sad little water stained box that'd you put maybe four things in and it'd be full. By that time, Dewy's crap was in a corner of my room which meant that those crazy Greens would not just be in my condo they would be in my *room*. For some reason, *all* of them had to come to fill and carry out that stupid box. It became a sort of weird ritual or something; the ritual of the tiny, water stained box. The mother would stare at Dewy's stuff and dab at her red eyes as her husband pulled at his beard. Pepi would sprawl on my bed and follow me around the room with her fevered eyes. I guess she expected me to fuck her right there with her father so close I could smell his cheap ass cologne. They'd pack that stupid little box and one of the parents would pause at the door before leaving.

*I know it's hard for you, too, Cobalt, but what did she say? When?*

*After they shot her.*

Not a thing.  Not a fucking thing.

I guess they were hoping I remember something. They still text me with that same question, it's been two years but I guess time is meaningless when your child gets killed.

After they'd leave I'd sit on my bed, watch stupid stuff online, and drink a lot.

I'd see Dewy staggering as the bullets hit her, see the pain in her mother's face--

Pepi lying there with her tits popping out of her shirt. That retard with the big cock in his hand.

And I'd see that dick filming my friend die with his phone: *I am gonna get paid, I am so gonna get paid.*

Someone in this bar told me that the guy who filmed Dewy left the city. The story was that Mr. Get Paid believed that the cops were following him because he filmed them gunning down an unarmed woman. Beyond that shit with the cops there has to be a downside to people thinking that you came into money--

Money changes shit, it changes how all the people in your life see you.

Even the people that love you see you differently, they can't help it.

Mr. Get Paid probably saw getting to film someone die in the same way my Dad sees winning the lotto. My Dad isn't a dick but he has his own stupid fantasies. What if he won the lotto? What if that shit happened for real? For one thing, my dad would shit his pants. He would really shit them, no joke. Luckily he could afford a hundred more of those track suits he loves, the satiny ones that are so shiny they sparkle under lights--

So, he'd buy a hundred more sets. At least.

The sad thing is that he would find himself alone. He has these fat, turgid sort of middle-aged bros he drinks cheap beer with. They play cards or watch sports as they drink case after case of nasty beer and fart and make all sorts of nasty jokes about nasty things.

It's horrible but it's also the center of my dad's life--

And it'd be gone.

All those guys who have known dad since I was in diapers would see him differently. It's not like they're bad people, they're actually decent guys, but that shit happens. All of them are just getting by just like everyone else I know--

What if all of the sudden one of them is rich?

That would have to be weird, maybe it would even piss you off. Why did your buddy luck out while you're still wallowing in shit? You have all these things you need, all of these things you make do without--do you hit your buddy up for some money? If you do the way things are between you changes. You become the small man, cap in hand, asking for help. Your buddy has the power and that sucks, makes you feel small, like less of a man. Even if you don't ask for help everything still changes. Your buddy isn't in a shitty apartment anymore, he doesn't want to keep drinking cheap ass beer and eating frozen burritos--he wants to do things and go places you can't.

There's no way a friendship can survive that.

I know how much those old assholes mean to my dad. The fucked up thing is that if I am aware of this then he must be also, right? I mean, I am half *him*, right? If I understand this then he must understand it, too; my dad must know that his dream coming true would mean a whole lot of unhappiness--what the fuck is up with that? I think about that shit a lot, my dad just getting older and fatter and sadder in this big house--just him and a hundred tracksuits.

# 8

Dewy didn't have to die that night. She could have smiled and been cool to that cop and no one would have ever known her name. Instead, she got caught in a moment that would rob her of forty or fifty years. Why did she do it? I was there and I have no idea. My guess is that D was tired and in a bad mood; maybe she'd had one too many shitty shifts at her shitty job. I was tired and didn't want to deal with facist cops but I knew not to fuck with them. What good does it do? Shit ain't gonna change. Dewy didn't go that deep, she didn't bother thinking what would happen to her--what would happen to all of us.
No, Dewy just felt her anger and reacted without thinking—
And it got her killed.
This is why I am so sick of everyone worshipping Dewy Green.
She wasn't some mighty symbol or whatever, she was just another person like you or me.
The only difference is that she did something stupid and got shot.

After D was killed all these book readers were disappointed that her death hadn't started a revolution. They were hoping that since a white woman was killed by the cops people would rise up and the world would change. The thing is, most people don't want the world to change. It may be a shitty world but it's the only one we know. We have learned to work within the shittiness and it is comforting in some fucked up way. Madras Mike is a horrible man, but he is a part of my life--same with my crappy condo. We all have shitty bosses and rent crappy places and those things make us who we are. Not just that but most people don't have it in them to do more than survive these days--

It's all just fucking pointless: *Thinking. Dreaming.*

# 9

I have to go by that stupid bus stop nearly every day. Every
once in awhile I almost tear up and have to check myself.
It's not because I lost a friend, it's more an awareness of
how fucked up things are. When people talk about how the
world can change it only reminds me that the world will
never get better.  I have fun, I go to bars and get trashed
and other shit but I never forget that there is this mess
around the edge of our lives. If you can't see it out of the
corner of your eye you can smell it, you can *hear* it. I am
really not some dark, sad person but Dewy's death put me
in touch with some shit I was only vaguely aware of
before. Sometimes I'm cool and I use it to make the good
times seem even better but sometimes I get this feeling in
my heart like a brick.

Dewy was close to my age--I want to say she was two
months older--so I saw someone my age die.  I watched her
eyes close, saw her chest stop rising and falling--
I felt her fucking go.
One second Dewy's body had a person inside it and the
next it was a blank, just a package of meat. I couldn't stop
staring at her body; I knew I had to get the fuck out of there
but some weird shit was going on.
Another bus came to take us away; I got on but in some
ways I didn't.
Sometimes I'll get off the bus to look at the spot where she
died.  Some stupid assholes always leave flowers and shit

there; the cops come and throw them in the trash but then more stupid assholes bring more flowers.

It's a ritual just like the Greens coming to pick up Dewy's crap in that sad, water stained box.

# 10

My parents are disappointed that I haven't gotten on one of those queer reality shows where queers do harmless shit like listen to ABBA and help clueless straights pick out clothes and decorate. I have a press pack: My parents hired someone to make one for me. They are broke ass, they couldn't even lend me money when I needed to have a tooth pulled, but they had the money to have a press pack made. I sent that press pack out to *Fruity Fabulous!* and *Butt Broz* and *Nancy Noez.*

Nothing.

That first round of failure meant nothing to my parents.

*We spent a lot on those kits, why aren't you using them?*

Each season I send them out to those same damn shows, my six year old press kit. I keep hoping they'll run out of them but my mom keeps finding more in the closet. I wonder if the people who fill roles on those shows recognize those old kits and think I'm insane.

*Oh my, God! That crazy queer sent us his old press kit again!*

I remember one night Dewy and I were chilling at the apartment, getting our drink on. She found my press kits and started laughing:

*You look like a mannequin, Cobalt! My God, that face; no wonder they didn't pick you!*

Dewy loved to bust my balls, sometimes I wonder if it was because I wouldn't fuck her. I've been with women a couple of times and stupidly shared that with Dewy once when I was drunk.

*You fucked her--is she better than me?*

*No, Dews. I don't know--it was weird, it just happened. We were drunk.*

*Aren't we weird?  Maybe you need to drink more.*

She got on my nerves sometimes, sometimes I wanted to ring that girl's neck--

Nowadays I lie on my bed half-hoping she'll walk in my room like the shooting never happened.

I'll smell her shampoo and cuss her out for spilling her nasty wine on my bed.

She spilled a whole glass a couple of days before she died. After the shooting I'd wrap the blanket around me to smell it…

I didn't wash that blanket until it started to get nasty. After a couple of times through the laundry the smell of wine--any traces of Dewy smells--vanished.

# 11

I get off at the bus stop where Dewy was shot without thinking. One second I'm on the bus messing with my phone and the next I'm standing on the sidewalk staring at the pavement where she fell. There's a corner grocery and a weird hippy store and these newer condos that are supposed to be really small inside. I have gone by that place so many times on the way to or from work that I could totally paint those condos and that corner store and that stupid hippy shop from memory. Someone sprayed "Get Up Off My Nutz" on the wall of the hippy shop and I guess the hippies are too lazy to clean it off.

Sometimes, I'll just smoke a cigarette and stare at the writing on that wall. There's no chalk outline where Dewy died, no trace of what happened except the footage that guy shot and the short movie in my head--

She was burned, I think; her parents were broke so the County burned her or something. Someone told me once that the ashes of charity cases are tossed in a landfill. What a thought, just drifting like snow over all the unfinished TV dinners and broken chairs and chipped coffee cups...

It's weird to think of that happening to someone you knew, makes you realize it could happen to any of us.

Each time I get off at that stop I look up at the windows of that building with the small condos. They had to have heard those shots, they were crazy loud. Did any of them look out their windows and see a plain girl with dark blonde hair lying in a big pool of blood?  I was there, I saw how fast someone can go from being alive and talking to just being a pile of meat--it made me believe in the soul.  I know how cheesy that sounds but people are totally different after they're dead, something has left them and there is this deep quiet about them.

It's weird to me all these people who think Dewy was this amazing person, it's kind of like they have made her alive again but not the same at all--
A character in a show or something.
Maybe Dewy *was* amazing but only in the way that all of us are amazing--the random shit we do and say and never really think about: Dewy trying to pick up queer guys and drinking that nasty Chill River Chablis.
*It's only five dollars, Cobalt!*
*Uh, yeah, sweetie, and it tastes like it.*
You know when you get drunk and run out of whatever you started drinking and you really want to keep drinking? You know the time when the liquor stores have closed and you'll drink any nasty shit?
Even in that state I would never drink Chill River Chablis. It was Dewy's jam, though, she drank a bottle of it every night.  When I think of D I think of Chill River Chablis and that big, green coat--her only coat. It had these huge pockets that were big enough to hold a purse or a nasty bottle of wine.  I wonder what happened to that coat? I'm sure they had to throw it out because of all the blood and stuff but I wonder if it is in a landfill or if they burned Dewy in it?  I have no idea how they do that shit--do they

burn people naked or just throw them in the fire however they were dressed when they died?
Dewy's parents never told me and I never asked.

This is rare for me. I don't usually get this deep, dwell on morbid shit. I like to think that nothing really bothers me but maybe I've been fooling myself. Something about getting in a fight, seeing that guy's face when he took a swing at me--
Normally I don't dwell on how ugly and stupid life really is but that fight in the bar has made me think about a lot of things: Dewy. My dad and his lottery obsession. How we're all trying to get by in this chipped and stained world.

# 12

When the rookie shot Dewy with that machine gun the back of her big, green jacket blew out--
I guess the bullets went right through her, she was just a little thing. D's face got all small and tight like it was shrinking as she staggered back three steps. My friend swayed like a drunk for a moment before sinking to the ground as if the bones in her legs had dissolved. Dewy still had her Wal-Mart badge on when she died; they wrote her up two days later when she didn't show up for her next shift. Our manager came up to me with all the fake-ass boss man he could slap on.

"Hey, Cobalt, where's your buddy? I'm gonna have to write her up for a no show."

"She's dead, Jordan."

"Dead? How is she dead?"

"Cops shot her."

He just stared at me for a moment, felt that was enough pity time, and plowed on.

"She has a Wal-Mart vest; can you bring it in?"

And that was all our boss had to say about Dewy Green being gunned down. It's just a stupid, mean world and fat assholes like Jordan live like a stain on it. All the people who think they revere Dewy, would they have stood between her and that gun?

Words are easy, it's actions that cost us.

Saying I love you is easy, loving people is hard.

Going over all this stupid shit has made me realize that I loved Dewy Green. I was probably one of her best friends but I didn't stand up to those cops, I just stood off to the side and watched her die.

Tonight feels like the night Dewy died--
Something about that fight, how violence came out of nowhere...
I keep seeing that guy's face and how it got all twisted and angry--how he looked like an enraged ape. They left the bar and I got another drink. People went back to talking and laughing and trying to get laid. When this drink is gone I'll have one more before walking back to the condo. After closing the door I'll put my keys in the bowl and look at the curtain walls of the unofficial bedroom. Tonight, like many times over the past two years, I'll just stand there like an idiot...
It didn't happen, right? If I open those curtains I'll see her there curled up
in what I called "the Dewy ball."
I've done that, pulled open those curtains and stared into the darkness, hoping that when my eyes adjusted I'd see her there.
After a few seconds I pull the curtains closed and go to bed.

I have a lot of talk for people who want stupid shit: The guy who filmed Dewy dying. My dad playing the lotto. I guess I have my own stupid fantasies, most of us do. *Most of us*--not Dewy.

And yet she is the one who got what a lot of people dream of: She's famous, a legend. All these people think she was this amazing person. She's even on t-shirts.

Most of us ordinary people don't get that.

Most of us are gone the moment we die; Dewy was *born* the moment she died.

A fictitious Dewy, an ideal--not the Dewy I knew and loved and miss more than I care to admit.

# What Peace Means to Us

## A Story For Those Who Survived

**The Seldom Dogs**

Written between 1 February 2016 and 9 November 2018
Music listened to: The Church, Radiohead, Al Stewart,
Gerry Rafferty

**Rage Room**

Written between 3 November, 2018 and 17 February, 2019
Music listened to: The Cure (*Pornography/*"Charlotte
Sometimes"), Joy Division (*Closer*), Siouxsie and the
Banshees (various)

**Today's Lesson**

Written between 9 March, 2018 and 16 May, 2019
Music listened to: Duran Duran ("My Antartica" "Too Late
Marlene," "Come Undone," "The Chauffeur")

**Golden Bullet**

Written in 2009
Music listened to: Nick Cave and the Bad Seeds, Depeche Mode

**Death Becomes Dewy Green**

Written between 1 February and 10 February, 2012
Music listened to: None (written on buses and trains)